The Book of Onei

The Book
Of Onei

ISBN: 978-1-7357944-9-5

Ritona
an imprint of RITONA a.s.b.l
3 Rue de Wormeldange
Rodenbourg, Luxembourg
L-6995

Layout and Design: Rhyd Wildermuth
View our catalogue and online journal at
ABEAUTIFULRESISTANCE.ORG

This book is an antinomian dream grimoire.

Oneiromancy, night wandering, mythic dreaming – by any name, dream magic is the art of traveling to the world of myth and wonder in dreams or half-dreams.

The things you do there, the quests you experience there, and the riddles you answer there are up to you. Your dreams are your own dreams, although some dreams are shared.

Nothing in this book should be taken literally. Nothing should be taken as a metaphor either.

Miracles and magic happen every single day but dream magic offers something much more wonderful than power – a secret that waits beyond dream and death.

Finding that secret is up to you, but it is the purpose of everything you'll find in this book.

Contents

THE ART OF NIGHT WANDERING
A Journey to Onei—10
Magic Harp-Strings—15
The Spider's Song—16
The Plain of Night—18
The City of the Gods—20
The Blue Desert—22
The Cliffs of Saint and Sage—24
What the Spider Said—26
Dead Leaves—28
Seven Levels of Dreaming—30
A Vade Mecum—31
On the Borders of the Night—32
A Journey to Onei (2)—33
To the Keeper of the Gate—35
Offering Prayer—36
The Three Types of Dreamers—37
Darkseer—38
The Powers of the First Darkness—39

THE LORE OF ONEI
When the Sons of the Crow Came Down on Onei—42
Sorrow of the Gorge—48
The Book—50
How Doubt Left the Empire—51
Lore of Onei—57
"Don't Question Heaven"—60
Darkness and Silence—61
The Country of the King—62
Under the Bright Dark—64
The Ship of Stars—65
A Journey to Onei (3)—67

THE POWERS OF ONEI
The Man Who Learned to Love the Law—71
The Veiled One—73
Boneyard Goddess—74
Death Barker—75
The Host—76
The Blood Wisdom—77
The Red Queen—78
The Secret of Solomon—80
The Wonder, the Horror, and the Art—82
The Majesty—84
The False Prophet—86
The Caesar Stones—87
Powers Glimpsed in Onei—88
The Story of the Man Who Learned to Love the Law—91
A Journey to Onei (4)—96

EXORCISM
The Three Types of Nightmare—99
The Blue Pearl Charm—100
Send the Dead to the Dead—101
Vampires—103
Transformation of Spirits—105
Power of Powers—106
Poppet-Binding Exorcism—108
The Gift of Horror—109
A Journey to Onei (5)—110

NIGHT HUNTING & WAR WIZARDRY
Sons of the Crow—113
Night Hunting—114
The War Figures—115
Binding—116
Antinomian—117
Night Hunters—118
Warding Spell—119

The Wild Hunt—121
A Journey to Onei (6)—123

DREAM ALCHEMY
The Fire and Water Scroll—126
Theory of Dream Alchemy—128
The Language of the Birds—129
The Five Operations—131
Dream Elixirs—133
Alchemical Correspondences—134
Dream Talismans—135
The Starry Powers—136
The Pharisee—139

DIVINATION AND PROPHECY
The Oracle—141
Greed—142
Divination by the Bones—143
The Armadel—144
Priest, Sage, or Magician—148
A Journey to Onei (7)—150

ABOUT THE AUTHOR—151

The Art of Night Wandering

A Journey to Onei

I was nearly forty years old when it first came over me, the strange feeling that I no longer knew myself. I was sitting in my own house at three in the morning, thinking back on the life I had lived. You start off with so many choices and then you start to pick between them, and every time you choose one path instead of another all your options start to narrow in. You become who you are, and it's easy to forget you could have been a lot of other things. You could have been once, but you no longer can. Now you are whatever you decided to be, and there are no more open vistas.

The whole house was asleep. You can only have thoughts like that in the first place when everyone else is asleep, because that's the only time when your mind is free enough. It's the only time when no one needs you.

I looked up at the fan blades as they turned and turned, and their long shadows flew across the ceiling like angelic messengers moving rapidly before the sun. My wife and my little daughter lay asleep in their beds, but I hadn't slept in at least three days.

What I was thinking as I was lying there is that yearning is everything. The whole structure of the universe is based on it. The craving for fulfillment is in every seed, reaching up for the untouchable sun. It's not an anomaly; it's right there in the blueprint. So when a little girl yearns for her mother, or a man for his lover, or a mystic for the god she serves, it's not some pathos to be cured. That suffering and that yearning and that loss is the fire of creation.

"Maybe we should take a trip to the mountains," my wife had said that morning, lying with her head up in the crook of my shoulder. She was trying to comfort me, trying to give me something to look forward to. But I wasn't sad, exactly.

"We are what we are," I answered her. "And we can't pretend. The dead come easily to us and the angels don't. How often do you see the shining ones? How often do you see the dead? You know what we are as well as I do. We are darkseers, not lightseers. I've been thinking a lot about the basement lately."

"I don't like it when you talk about the basement," she said, and pulled back to look at me. The basement is where the door is.

So there I was, sitting up awake and alone at three in the morning, not at all certain how it got this way, how I ended up who I am. I watched the fan blades as they turned and turned, and a strange memory came over me. A strange hunger began to grow inside me, not completely unfamiliar and yet almost forgotten. I stood up silently and slipped my shoes on and went downstairs, moving quietly so as not to wake my wife up. Not only was the door down there (though it had long gone unused) but the book was too—The Book of Onei, my father's crime.

The steps creaked as I walked on them, and the dead things whispered. The basement was where he had kept them bound, and they wouldn't like my interference. But what else can you do with the dead? After all, you can't kill them.

I took a match out and I lit the lamp and rummaged around in boxes until I found the book. The door in the corner shuddered angrily, but I took the book out anyway.

The ancient chaos, the primal darkness. That was the answer to it all. My father had stolen this book from the Great Library of Onei, and the weight of that shadow had hung over us like an evil cloud. But I wasn't convinced that what he did was wrong. Who are the Great Ones to withhold this knowledge?

The dead responded a few nights later. I had brought The Book of Onei up from the basement where it had slept for years. I had read aloud from its forbidden pages. I had begun to compose a few poems of my own about the dreams and the darkness, loose tributes to demonic geniuses such as Li Ho and Meng Chiao. I had even added a few of them to The Book of Onei.

In reading from the book and in composing those poems I had upset a fragile peace. The things in the basement slipped their bonds, which were only ever made of a certain mindset— a mindset I had not maintained. They came floating up after me late one night while I lay there staring at the ceiling in the lonely hours, believing myself to be wide awake.

My daughter stirred in her sleep and moaned. My wife opened her eyes. The whole house was permeated with a sickening dread, the presence that makes your skin crawl and the hair on the back of your neck stand up. The light in the kitchen blinked on and off. Deep in my stomach, nausea stirred.

"You're going to do what your father did, aren't you?" said my wife. "You're going to go through the door."

I nodded in the darkness of early dawn. "I've done it before," I told her. "Before you and I were together. But I haven't seen Onei in years."

"You're going over there to steal something."

"Yes, of course. That's what my father did, and it's what I'll do too. The things in the basement are getting restless, because they can sense the way I've been feeling lately. My father always said it was an evil book, that it had cursed him ever since he took it. But that's not what I believe."

"Why not?" she asked, a little harshly. "You're endangering us all!"

"I think it scared him so much that he misunderstood it. He always told me that the dead things followed him over from Onei when he brought back the book, and that they were always warning him not to read it, not to use it, not to learn from it. But the primal darkness is the source of wisdom. He stole its secrets and then feared to read them, so he bound the dead up with spiderweb thoughts and left them down there to haunt his dreams. They made his last years one endless nightmare. I don't want that to happen to me. I don't want it to happen to my daughter either. She'll inherit the book."

"You could return the book," she pointed out. "You could bring it back to the Great Library of Onei. Then the dead would leave us alone."

"I'm not even sure that's true. There is such a thing as retribution. And that would only make what he suffered completely meaningless. Prometheus didn't give the fire back."

"And look what happened to him! So what exactly are you going to do?"

"I'm going to learn how to use it. My father was never able to use the book, because he didn't understand it, he didn't know why it was so important to the dead. That is the knowledge I intend to steal."

She was silent for a long time. The sun rose outside, and in the pale light my daughter stirred. She would soon be awake.

"How long will you be gone?" my wife asked. Her voice shook a little.

"Not long at all. I'll be back before the sun finishes rising."

"Or else you won't be back. Not ever again." I didn't answer her that time. There's no answer to the truth.

So I went down to the basement again and I heard the voices, whispering the things they always whisper, the threats and the warnings. I walked through the gauntlet of the voices as if they could not daunt me, although I was going into their place of strength. I had the book in my backpack. The door at the end of the basement jumped angrily as I approached it, rattled a few times, then settled in. I put my hand on the doorknob, said a prayer to the protecting powers, and paused for a moment in silent thought. Then I walked through into the land of Onei.

Magic Harp-Strings

Clouds roll across a purple sky.
The witch pours out a cup.
The orange coals of incense burn.
She knows the goblins, how they yearn
To come and eat us up.

The wind cries out as if it's drunk.
The gods will soon be here.
The witch prepares a plate of meat.
The spirits come, and as they eat
She turns away in fear.

The Presence takes her, and her eyes
Roll up into her head.
Like passing clouds the spirits trace
Their shapes across her dreaming face,
The scriptures of the dead.

The gods are here, they're always here,
Although they are not seen.
They walk across the purple skies
Or in a witch's staring eyes
Or somewhere in between.

The Spider's Song

In the city of Sophia in the land of Onei, only wisdom was valued and the foolish were outcasts. The wise used them only for pulling carts or breaking stones, but those whose foolishness was too offensive to the wise were driven away, forced out into the rocky wasteland on the borders of the Plains of Day and Night. Sometimes the lights from their campfires could be seen in the distance, but this sight made the wise uneasy and so they often chose to leave their shutters drawn. All over the splendid city made of colored glass and hammered bronze, onion-domed towers and lofty pinnacles, the night was dark, but in the rocky wasteland outside the city there were lights like distant stars. It was almost as if the wise were frightened of those campfires, which grew more numerous every year.

Such a fate was Aphron's, son of the philosopher Qaran the Luminous. He had always been foolish, a drinker of strong wines and a sleeper at noon, but his father's reputation for wisdom was so pronounced, even in a city as wise as this one, that he had managed to reach his nineteenth year before anyone dared to speak against him. When the outcry to banish Aphron came at last, his father Qaran took him aside and sought to prepare him for what lay ahead.

"My son," he said, "you are not wise, but there is no need for you to become one of those who cluster around the campfires at the edge of the city. For there are two paths to wisdom, and one is close at hand. If you go out past the rocky wasteland

and into the Plains of Day and Night, you will come to the Starry River. Cross that river, and seek the priests in the Plain of Day. They will teach you the wisdom of faith and service, and you may return here as a priest."

So Aphron set off, and his path took him out through the rocky wasteland and past the ashes of the discarded cooking fires. None of the foolish were to be seen by day, and rumor had it that they shunned the daylight, seeking to hide their shame by burrowing and digging, living in caves like furtive animals. It took Aphron three days to cross the rocky wasteland, but he never saw any fools there, only their campfires after sunset. When he made an effort to approach a campfire, it would wink out like a closing eye, leaving the night in a more total darkness. So Aphron concluded that the fools had rejected him, knowing him somehow to be a seeker of wisdom. He pressed on into the Plain of Night.

The Plain of Night

The Plain of Night was a terrible place, where the sun never rose and the moon never shone, like the moonless nights preferred by thieves and reivers. No path showed the way through that dark, flat plain, but for as long as Aphron walked upon it he heard noises in the nearer distance. Stealthy footsteps crept slowly up on him, seeming to be preparing an ambush, but no predator ever struck. Sinister whispers seemed to breathe conspiracies, but he could never make out the words they were speaking. The fear of walking through constant danger was far worse for Aphron than an actual attack, for as a frequenter of taverns and wine houses he was no stranger to sudden violence, and he carried a long, flame-bladed rapier at his side. He clutched the hilt and prepared himself, but no attack ever came.

Without any sign of sun or moon, he had no idea how long he walked, but at last he came to a shining river, faintly silver with the light of all the constellations that seemed to glow from beneath the waters. Aphron could not decide if there were stars in the water, the night sky of some other world perhaps, or if it was only a reflection. When he compared the constellations in the Starry River to those in the sky above him, they did not seem quite the same, but he was at a loss to say exactly how. Remembering that he was a fool after all, he gave up wondering, and looked for a place to cross the river.

There was a ferry-man on the riverside in the silvery darkness, sitting and playing dice with no one and drinking dust from an old clay cup. When he looked up at Aphron and spread his hand for the fare, his smile looked as evil as a death's head grinning, and his skin was stretched so tight over his bones he might as well have been a skeleton. But after Aphron had paid the fare, and the two of them had gone halfway across the river, his flesh filled out. His malicious grin became a somber frown, he grew a long white beard, and his eyes became bright and blue, though they stared blindly ahead of him. A moment later, they passed into daylight. Before the ferry-boat had crossed the Starry River, both sides of the bank had been the same black landscape. Now both of them were all but drowned in sunlight, and the Plains were a wonderland of grass and flowers, while the air was so fresh it tasted like honey. The ferry-boat landed on the Plain of Day, and Aphron walked in search of the priests who live there.

The City of the Gods

The City of the Gods in the Plain of Day was home to many temples, and the creed they taught was one of love and service—love for the gods and service to humanity. The priests of the Plain of Day were not corrupt, but genuine servants who strove only to stand as interpreters between the earth and heaven, and who trained the priests of the many cities of Onei in the subtle intricacies of the celestial language. Aphron the Fool sought out the temple of Wisdom, for the goddess of Wisdom was the goddess of his city, and no man who had learned her mysteries would ever be accounted a fool.

"The highest wisdom," the priest told him, "Is the wisdom of discernment, which will allow you to serve both god and man. And the key to discernment is to learn the flavor—the taste and the texture of wrong and right. First I will feed you the wrong."

The priest gave him something that looked much like chocolate, the richest and darkest of chocolates, but its taste was sour. It was the taste of his mouth on a long and hateful morning after too much wine the night before, the sweat of an anonymous lover's unloved flesh, the iron-like stench of blood on his blade after a misspent word.

"I know this taste," he said. "And it is poisonous. Because of these flavors I was sent into exile."

"Then consider that your first taste of wisdom. Now I will feed you the right."

What the priest fed him now was like an amber-colored honey, the taste of goodness and piety, the taste of loving kindness. For many days he feasted upon it, because the taste was new to him, and at first it seemed to Aphron to be the greatest joy he had ever known. For one month and then three months and for one year and then three years, Aphron fed only on the honey of righteousness. But then in time it began to pall. The taste it left in his mouth was so sweet as to be nauseating, and he longed for something more solid to feast upon.

"Honey is sweet," he said. "But it is not satisfying."

The high priest sighed, and opened a door that led out of the temple. "In that direction is the Blue Desert. If you can cross its sand dunes and survive its dangers, you will come in time to the Cliffs of the Sages. They teach the other path to wisdom."

And the high priest would not look at him, but would only point ahead at the Blue Desert with his face averted, as if Aphron had disappointed him or possibly shamed him somehow. So Aphron set out on the road again, two times an exile.

The Plain of Day was filled with temples, and Wisdom was only one of them. There were temples to all of the gods on the Plain of Day, from the lordly and wrathful Thunder Wolf to the Huntress with her bow and arrows. He stopped at none of them, though a man could learn wisdom by studying at any of them. The path of the priests was not for him.

The Blue Desert

On the third day after he left the Temple of Wisdom, Aphron reached the end of the Plain of Day. Blue sands of a darkly luminous color stretched out to the edge of the horizon and beyond, like an ocean without a drop of water in it. Aphron walked on into the Blue Desert without giving the City of the Gods another thought.

The Blue Desert was a dangerous place. The sands in the Blue Desert had a mysterious color, that deep yet still luminous color of the last minutes of twilight. This color is usually seen only in the twenty minutes or so before true nightfall, when the sun has gone down completely but the sky has not yet forgotten what the daylight used to be. It is the color of melancholy, the type of melancholy that is aesthetically pleasing, an emotion as hypnotic and fatal as the eyes of a cobra.

As he crossed the Blue Desert on foot, Aphron succumbed to that melancholy, suddenly swept by a terrible longing that yet seemed indescribably beautiful to him. He was thinking about a former lover from the City of Wisdom, a great beauty whose eyes had shined with much the same color (or so it seemed to him now). He suddenly decided he must have been in love. He couldn't know this, of course, but they had already driven his former lover out, to join the other fools whose camp-fires dotted the rocky wasteland. This twilight-eyed beauty was far from tortured by thoughts of Aphron (being rather more concerned with immediate survival), but Aphron was suddenly tortured by thoughts of them.

If torture is really the right word for it, that is—because it had much to savor in it, this emotion of yearning and loss and poignant memory. He thought about their blue eyes, the same blue as the sands, and the soft waves of their long wheat-colored hair. He thought about the way they smiled at him when he came into the tavern, and the way they sang for him when the two of them were alone. These thoughts were painful—among the worst pain he had ever experienced—but he would sooner have given an arm than give them up, and that is never true of anything we do not crave. Aphron craved his own suffering, and for as long as he craved his suffering, he wandered aimlessly through the desert.

No one can say how long he wandered there, but Aphron was a fool—and no fool ever kept the face of one lover before his eyes for very long. He savored the beauty of his own suffering for a time that felt terrible, and he could have sworn that it was a hundred years - and then another old infatuation crossed his mind, a red-headed fruit seller he had met for just as long as it took him to buy some peaches. As soon as he thought of this fact, he laughed, and as soon as he laughed at his own foolishness, the blue sands lost their power. The Cliffs of Saint and Sage were right there in front of him, a walk of no more than a few hours.

The Cliffs of Saint and Sage

When he arrived at the cliffs, their height was terrifying, but he could see that there were people who lived on them in caves like birds. There were piles of bones below the cliffs, as of people who fell, but he couldn't tell if they were the saints and the sages or merely would-be visitors who had tried to climb up to them. There was no way to reach the caves except to climb the cliffs, so Aphron disregarded the risk and began to climb.

Three times he almost fell and joined the bleached bones at the bottom, but each time he caught a hold and continued to climb. He reached a cave before nightfall, and the old hermit who lived in the cave was clearly a sage. He looked on Aphron with eyes that burned, and gestured for him to crawl into the cave.

"I have long awaited you," he said. "Twice-exiled Aphron the Fool. You rejected the path of the priests, because the priests know nothing except right and wrong. Wrong and right are merely opposites, and the path of the sage is to transcend such opposites. By rejecting the path of the priest, you have begun the journey. To complete it, you must wear this hair-shirt, and live in this cage on the side of the cliff. When you no longer know of hot and cold, like or dislike, good or bad, you will have become a sage."

So Aphron lived in the cage on the side of the cliff, praying and meditating and starving and itching. He understood the purpose of it—which made him wonder whether he was really such a fool as he had always been told—but the hair shirt scratched him and burned him, and the cold winds that swept the side of the cliff made him shiver, and the occasional bird's egg the hermit fed him was less than nourishing. He felt his mind changing as the days wore on, but not in the way the hermit intended. He wasn't piercing the veil between right and wrong. He wasn't transcending his preferences. He was only becoming strange, sinking down into a deeper foolishness in which he thought he could begin to understand the language of the spiders, the music that sunlight makes, and the logic of the clouds.

The hermit pulled his cage in one day for the purpose of feeding him, saw the crazed look in his eyes, and began to beat him with an old bone. Aphron chose not to resist this violence, but it did make him wonder. How was it that a sage could become so angry?

What the Spider Said

As he lay in the bottom of the cage on the side of the cliff, a black widow spider crawled up to him. The spider said this: "Soon to be thrice-exiled, you are one of my kind, a follower of the third path. For there are priests and there are sages, but there are also magicians. The priest serves the community through prayer and sacrifice, through articulating its deepest values, and by mediating between god and man. The sage, on the other hand, makes men into gods, by teaching them the wisdom to stand as high as heaven. The magician does neither."

"Then what does the magician do?" asked Aphron. And the spider sang:

In the ruined walls of Carthage
There's a man who sits alone.
He can tell you what your dream is
From the cracks along a bone.

In the Empty Quarter, keening,
There's a woman, old and blind,
And her milky eyes are staring
Through Saharas of the mind.

They will show you how to do things-
How to rule the wind and storm.
But you'll find yourself a stranger
In the place where you were born.

As the spider completed this mysterious song, the hermit heard him, and came rushing forward with a little knife. "You've been listening to the spiders," he said, "Just like the others!" And the hermit cut the rope, sending Aphron the Fool to his death far below.

Or such was his intention. For while most of those who heard the spider's song had gained too much wisdom, leading them to contemplate their own deaths with a fatal dispassion, Aphron had only become more strange. He had achieved the foolishness of poetry and of the wandering stranger, and the laws of the world held no weight with him. He changed into a crow with a flick of his thoughts, flew out between the bars of the cage, and disappeared into the open sky.

"Where are you going?" yelled the hermit, waving his knife at the departing bird. "Where are you going, you fool?"

"I fly for Carthage," croaked the bird.

Dead Leaves

I step outside. It's true, perhaps—the years
Have folded me, transmuted me, and made
A different man. The mix of light and shade

With which I started is, no doubt, the same
And yet the shape is altered. I have come
So far, this time, from where I started from

It feels like transmigration. And my self
Can't quite recall the self it used to be.
I look up, feeling old and lost, and see

A sky of midnight blue. The clouds roll past.
The dead leaves whisper. In the rising wind
Are hints of what I thought I'd left behind.

I used to know a way out. That's a truth,
Though not a fact, exactly. There's a feat-
You don't ignore the facts. You merely cheat.

And still they call me—shadows from the fire
That burns behind the door. The dark, red wine
Of knowing how to walk the borderline.

I turn and go inside. Tonight I'll dream
And slip through boundaries, past seas of glass
And mountains hot as blood and dead as ash.

Prometheus and I, we share a knack
For abstract theft. And though it's been too long,
Still, "Whom the gods destroy." You know the song.

Seven Levels of Dreaming

1—the mundane
2—the curious
3—the mythic
4—the mysterium
5—a vision
6—an epiphany
7—annihilation

Mundane dreams are those that come in through the Gates of Ivory; they contain no magic.

Curious dreams are intermingled with hints and glimpses of magic.

Mythic dreams come in through the Gates of Horn; they are dreams of true and sacred things presented in the form of myth.

Dreams of the mysterium involve magic power, a drunken electric ecstatic presence.

Visions display the vividness and intensity of the Phantasia Catalyptica.

Epiphanies answer great riddles and questions.

Annihilation destroys the dream. That which waits here is the same as that which waits beyond death.

A Vade Mecum

1—Seek out darkness and silence.

2—Drift on the river of sleep and daydream.

3—Hear what the voices tell you; see what you see.

4—Record all glimpses of Onei, in daydream or night-dream.

5——Answer all riddles; complete all quests.

As hard at it can be to enter Onei intentionally, it is always possible to walk the Borderlands - the place in your mind between sleep and waking, between Earth and Onei.

Spirits, dreams and messages from Onei will find you there.

On the Borders of the Night

I've lived here on the borders of the night,
Where dark divides from light.
I've walked the marches made of fire and snow.

Each night I lock the doors and close my eyes
To watch the rivers rise.
I've tasted all those memories—I know.

Though there are things that I can never mend,
If I could choose again
I'd take the path I took so long ago.

A Journey to Onei (2)

Crossing over into the borders of Onei, I saw a thick and shadowy forest. It's always like that, by which I mean there is always a barrier—not that there is always a forest. And this forest was deep, as deep as the waters of a still, black lake without a wind to ruffle its surface. I heard no birds, felt nothing but a malevolent watchfulness. At the edge of the trees there stood a pair of pillars, guarded by two grinning and silent skulls. The dead stared back at me in blind resentment. I was alive and they were not, and that's more than enough.

The guardian sat there dressed in red, its face obscured behind a cloud of smoke. It nodded solemnly as I approached, waiting to see if I knew the invocation. The heads in the pillars had failed to give it, which is ironic of course. You compose it yourself.

I opened my copy of the Book of Onei, turned to a blank page, and began to speak. The words of my invocation appeared on the page in red and black. I know I said that I could hear no birds, but as soon as I had finished speaking a great flock arose, flying in rapid and violent circles about the nimbus of the sun.

The guardian stood, its robes the color of a thick red wine. It made a gesture with its hands, an ancient symbol I had never seen before but which I recognized immediately. What it meant was "proceed," and it obliged the heads to stop their silent laughter.

It had no such power over the forest, which continued to brood in malicious silence. I knew my own tendency toward a violent melancholy and didn't take it personally.

In a clearing between the trees that night I dug a pit with my hands, a place for offerings to the underworld powers. The pit was like a gaping mouth, a waiting throat, opening wide in eager wetness to devour the world. I lit a fire in front of it, honoring the powers of the empty heavens. The celestial deities, the stars and planets, the vast, blue void with its howling winds—I made my offerings to all that beauty, all that horror and all that wonder.

And then I crouched in silence, waiting for the spirits to render their judgement. I remembered a dream. The night when the Host came was a terrible night, perhaps the night that had driven me here. There is no horror like that horror, unthinking and childlike, the knowledge that there is something beyond death—and that it knows who you are. They almost had me that time, but I turned out to not be as powerless as the Host believed me.

I had my knowledge, the lore my father had stolen from Onei. He gave that power to me, though he had never dared to use it himself. I made a sign with my fingers, I broke the glamour of the wrathful dead…

And that was my answer from the forest spirits: "The darkseer needs no permission to journey on into Onei."

To the Keeper of the Gate

A prayer with offerings to gain entrance to the Borderlands:

Phantoms of the forest gather
In the shadows of the trees.
Hidden voices whisper, whisper.
I have come for all of these.

Praises to the guardian spirit,
Keeper of the in-between.
There are ways that I must wander,
And you know what ways I mean.

Here beneath the bone-white birches
And the blue-green spruce and pine
I have brought you bowls of chicken,
Goblets filled with rich red wine.

Spirit of the borders, hear me.
Throw the doors of twilight wide.
Tell the skulls that guard the pillars,
Grant me leave to pass inside.

Offering Prayer

Burn the appropriate candle and recite this prayer when you leave an offering to the powers:

*This hungry pit shall open wide
And gorge on meat and wine.
These flames will burn as night-clouds turn
To watch this work of mine.*

*This shaft will gape so none escapes
Its toothless maw tonight.
While blue-white stars look down in awe
To see the flames so bright.*

*Oh gods of endless space and sky,
Oh gods of underneath,
Oh gods who live and gods who die
And gods who wait beneath,*

*Accept these morsels from my hand,
Drink deep and eat your fill.
I seek no benefits tonight
Unless you share my will.*

The Three Types of Dreamer

Lightseers—night wanderers who most easily or frequently contact celestial and benevolent entities.

Earthseers—dreamers who dream true things, but of Earth and not of Onei.

Darkseers—night wanderers who most easily or frequently contact cthonic and horrifying entities.

Darkseer

It's not that the blue-green mountains don't appeal.
I can feel their majesty,
Their sense of distance.
It's just that there's also something else —
For instance,
The something wicked that this way comes
In the witching hour,
The drunken trembling of branch and stem
And the formless Power.
And if I should sometimes prefer
To attach myself
To some beautiful chaos-
I can pay what it costs.

The Powers of the First Darkness

Alone at night, I hear the doorknob turn,
The hinges creak—and standing in the light
Are cold and silent men. I stand in fright,

And one by one they float in through the door.
Their suits are charcoal gray, their ties are thin.
On every mouth, a Mona Lisa grin.

Their eyes could just as well be balls of glass,
Their faces stuffed and mounted. Waves of dread
Pass over me and through me. Like the dead

There's nothing there at all—an absent space
Just papered over by a face as clean
And free of comment as a pure machine.

"We've found him," says the first one
And I turn, to try to get away. The power comes
And lifts me off my feet, completely numb

From crown to sole. Cold, drunken currents flow
And hold me in a field of fearful awe.
They know the truth. I disobeyed the Law
And now the consequence has found me out.

"You should have kept your mouth shut," says a voice,
"Or joined the Legion while you had the choice,

"But chronicling our secrets…" As I scream,
Their faces start to glow. They circle in
Like feeding sharks. But, though I may have sinned

I still remain defiant. Down below,
In Death's primeval waters, there is lore
Of hidden things that none have known before,

And I can steal it if I slip the trap.
The horror closes in. My fingers make
A sign of power, and I bolt awake.

My wife's asleep beside me in our bed.
The kitchen light is flickering. Outside,
The city sleeps. And I am still alive.

The Lore of Onei

When the Sons of the Crow Came Down on Onei

When the Sons of the Crow came down on Onei, the terror of their first appearance was like the rising of a blood-red star. Their eyes were feral and vengeful, and they were clothed in rags, black tatters like the wings of crows. Their fury lit first upon the City of Wisdom, which they destroyed completely in seven days. Men said that the Sons of the Crow were the fools of the wasteland, driven out from the City of Wisdom and returned now to take their vengeance, but none could say for certain. The Sons were like howling furies when they went into battle, and the wise could do nothing but die before them.

The Sons of the Crow were led by a prophet, a man who wore a long black crow's mask to hide his face. The name of the prophet was Eyes Like Flowers, and the heads of huge sunflowers spilled out from the eye-holes in his black mask, so that none could tell how he could see.

There was a story about Eyes Like Flowers, but none could say if it was true or not. According to the story, the prophet was originally a common criminal, arrested for inciting a riot in the streets of the city. When the wise men of the city declared his death sentence, he only laughed strangely at them but would say nothing. They tied him to a stake and prepared the bonfire, and the man who would soon lead the Sons of the Crow began to sing. His voice was like the harsh screech of a cawing crow.

When my eyeballs bloom like flowers
And my hands go forth to war,
When the bell that tolls the hours
Cracks and falls and rings no more…

According to the legend, Eyes like Flowers became a prophet as he sang the song. Gigantic sunflower heads burst out through his eye sockets, and his eyeballs fell out just like little glass marbles. His hands burst into flame even though the city Headsman had not yet lit the match, and the bonds with which they had tied his wrists burned black and snapped off.

The clock on the great brass tower in the center of the city, a beautifully complicated mechanism of gears and dials, had just been ringing the hour of noon. As Eyes Like Flowers sang the words of his song, the bell in the clock-tower suddenly cracked, falling to the ground in an explosion of bricks and splintered wood.

Across the length of Onei, on the Blue-Green Ocean, a hot wind began to blow. The sun blazed like a malignant eye, and the drought began that destroyed the Pearl States. By the end of that decade, large sections of the Blue Green Ocean had been boiled away to desert, gleaming whitely like a plain of salt.

As Eyes Like Flowers sang his song, the Wise - who had been watching his intended execution from a nearby balcony - had their crimes laid bare before the people of Sophia, appearing as flickering images on the passing clouds. Qaran the Luminous, the great philosopher, was exposed as an embezzler of the city funds. Tendress the High Priestess was shown taking bribes from the wealthy to preach whatever they wanted her to preach. Setnel the Astronomer had stolen another man's greatest discovery, then had his rival denounced as a fool and driven out into the wasteland.

It went on and on, and the people of the city were enraged by what they saw. The rioting that followed lasted for three days and four nights. Eyes Like Flowers disappeared, only to return at the head of his black-clad horde some ten years later. But all of this was only a legend, because no one outside the Sons of the Crow could say for certain, and the Sons of the Crow did not answer questions.

What is known is this. The prophet who was known as Eyes Like Flowers wore a crow mask with a long black beak, and long tattered robes that looked like crow's wings. In the eye-openings of his mask, there were giant sunflowers. When the Sons of the Crow came out from the wasteland, he got up in front of them and sang this song:

And are we not of the sons of the crow,
Who worship a hidden creed?
Or those who seek but do not know,
And hear, but do not heed?

When they heard these words, his followers howled, and the frenzy of their bloodlust blotted out all other sounds. Man and woman, young and old, the Sons of the Crow held their spears on high, while their commanding officers held curved white scimitars. The Wise of Sophia sent out their army, but the army was massacred before the gates of the city. Those gates were barred, but the Sons of the Crow laid siege to the walls.

The people of the back streets rose in rebellion, slaughtered the guards that held the gates, and threw them open to the Sons. They say the light from the flames could be seen in Qotar, but Qotar is more than two hundred miles away from what are now the ruins of the City of Wisdom.

That too is mere legend, but this is not: when the Sons of the Crow came down on Onei, the terror of their first appearance was like the rising of a blood-red star. From city to city and from land to land, the Sons of the Crow brought blood and fire. No one knew what they wanted, and none could say what they believed, for their Prophet spoke only in riddles and poetry. To the High Priest of the Adoration in the Plain of Day, Eyes Like Flowers sang these words:

I climbed a staircase to the land of birds
And told them what I'd learned.
They didn't care.
To birds, the world is made of clouds and air.

And then he inexplicably spared the Temple of Adoration from destruction by his horde, though the Temple of Wisdom was torn brick from brick and its priests impaled before the ruined walls.

Believing that the worship of Adoration must be favored somehow by the Sons of the Crow, thousands and thousands of people converted to that creed, and the whole land between what was once Sophia and what would someday be the Qalina became a stronghold of that faith. The Sons of the Crow did not always march, but disappeared into the deserts and the mountains for years at a time, reappearing to burn and kill. Yet when they did so, they showed no favor to any, burning the cities of the Adoring just as readily and as ruthlessly as any other.

When the fear of the Sons of the Crow had become too great to endure, and the fact that they favored no faith had become too obvious to ignore, a prophet arose from among the ranks of the Adoring. He was known as the Flagbearer, and he carried a flag before him into battle instead of any kind of weapon. All his followers did the same. The followers of the Flagbearer refused to fight, but only carried their flags ahead of them and stood before the Sons of the Crow. They died in their thousands, surrendering their own lives willingly as a shame and a rebuke. When the Flagbearer stood before Eyes Like Flowers, the mad prophet broke down and wept, singing these words as he fell to his knees:

> *We come to you with broken beaks*
> *And wings like crippled birds.*
> *It's better not to even speak*
> *Than lose the weight of words.*

Then all the Sons of the Crow dropped down to their knees, and their spears and their scimitars fell out of their hands. Their eyes were wet with sorrow and remorse, and the terror of their own damnation. But the Flagbearer replied with kindness:

On bended knee I sought the source
Of all that moves above,
And only when I knew remorse
Decided it was love.

The awful kindness of the Flagbearer shamed the Sons of
the Crow so that they took their own lives, unable to live with
the horror that they had made. And so the Flagbearer saved the
lands that would become the Qalina, the Empire of the Adoration. Yet he was not to be honored, for the priests of the Adoration could never trust him. He had no blood on his hands, but
the shame he inspired, the example of a thrilling and terrible
love, had destroyed an entire army. And so they had him
burned alive, and his followers scattered to the corners of the
earth.

There were those who disapproved, but one old man who
witnessed the execution nodded solemnly as the flames rose
high. As he turned away from the pile of ashes, he was heard to
say this:

He told me he could teach the art
The world was built upon.
And yet, within my secret heart,
I smiled when he was gone.

Sorrow of the Gorge

A shock of light above the gorge,
One moment of the sun.
The cliffs are like a closing mouth
Of frozen rock, and north and south
The frigid waters run.

I pause and glance ahead. The path
Is vertical and thin.
An ancient, rusted chain is here,
I wrap it round my hand in fear.
It bites into my skin.

The roots and boulders, tangled thick
As fingers intertwined,
Jut out as sharp as broken bones.
I cross a heap of ancient stones
And pour out half my wine.

"Come out and taste the wine," I call,
"Come out and drink your fill."
The wind comes roaring through the trees
And something in me dimly sees
The spirits of the hill.

I light an incense-stick and bow.
"I know it's cold up here.
The world has changed, and we have come
To hate the things we started from,
The magic and the fear.

"The face of death is hid behind
This horror we have made.
But fools prefer what's clear and bright.
They turn their backs on every sight
Of mingled light and shade.

"Still, there are things we owe the ghosts.
And some do not forget."
A mournful bird came floating by.
The mountain ghosts did not reply.
They haven't answered yet.

The Book

There is a book in Onei that contains all knowledge, including the knowledge of first things. If you are given access to the Book it can be a blessing or a curse.

I opened up the Book to find the place
That spoke of ancient things. My hands were cold,
My lips were purple. And the lamp was old—

It guttered angrily and cast off smoke
That stained my fingers black. I found the page
And what it said was this—"There was an age

In which the sun and moon, though dimly white,
Gave off no heat. Like lifeless rocks they hung
Above a world where primal darkness clung

And in that darkness, there were moving things
Like giant, hungry shadows. In the deep
That ancient chaos still remains asleep."

When the sun and the moon still gave no warmth,
and maneating giants still roamed the earth.

How Doubt Left the Empire

The Empire of the Adoration, also known as the Qalina, grew up out of the chaos left behind them by the Sons of the Crow. The Sons of the Crow destroyed the City of Wisdom and the City of the Gods, then disappeared into the Blue Desert for several years. They came out of the Blue Desert to destroy the City of the Sublime, where the worshipers of the Sublime had rebuilt their temples. They retreated for seven years into the Brokentooth Mountains, then came down again to burn several more cities.

The Flagbearer and his followers had stopped them, but the Flagbearer had been burned alive, because the priests of the Adoration did not trust his purity. Then the Temple of the Adoration became the ruler of the ruined lands, and imposed its teaching on every community. The Qalina was its High Priestess and its absolute ruler, and her followers believed in the legend of the Adoration: how it was he who brought the sun from the depths of outer space and installed it above the primal waters, how he pulled the ghosts of which people were made from out of the heart of a dying star in order to populate his new-made world, how he imprisoned the Chaos Worm beneath the same primeval ocean before calling up the islands and continents from beneath the waves, and how he saved his beloved people from being murdered by the vengeful stars, before imprisoning the stars in their cells in the firmament.

All believed, and no one questioned. But there was one who doubted, not the faith itself, but his own ability to live up to it. People called him the Doubtful, and they used to chase him through the streets and throw things at him. The priests would question him when he came to the temple, asking him why he doubted the faith. But he would deny that he doubted, saying only this:

> *Though he split the land from the water,*
> *Though he put each star in its own true place*
> *Though he spared us all from the slaughter*
> *I fear his face.*

"Fear and wisdom are closely connected," said a kindly priestess, washing the offal from off of his face. "You have the makings of a priest." But he shook his head, and the expression of fear on his face contained a tincture of a doubt, and so the priestess drove him out.

From the depths of his terrified heart, the Doubter bargained, holding his hands up to heaven in a pouring rain. He wanted to serve the Adoration, and he wanted to love him, but the possibility of the one seemed to render the other meaningless. No man can bargain with heaven, so his prayers were not answered. The priests of the Adoration demanded a goodness of which he knew he was not capable. This would not have hurt him, except that he knew his neighbors, and though all of them were pious, none of them were capable of true goodness either. This one was an adulterer and this other one a gossip, this one cheated at card games and still another was a drunk.

And as for the Doubtful, he had killed a man, though it was a long time ago and in another city far away.

He knew his own crime was a heavy one, but the church demanded a facade of piety, and this was something of which he did not feel capable. And so he sank deeper into doubt and despair, wandering along the roads of the Qalina and sleeping wherever the night surprised him.

He awoke one morning on the side of the road, as the cold light of a white dawn drained the darkness from the sky. There was a black crow standing on top of him, perhaps considering if he was dead enough to make a meal.

"Don't take my eyes," he said. "I am not yet ready."

The crow cawed once at him and flew away, but the Doubtful was disturbed by what he had seen in its eyes. For just a few seconds, before the crow flew away, weird images had flickered there like dim reflections: a blind old woman singing in a lifeless desert as vast as the world, a madman tracing the cracks in a human thighbone between the walls of a ruined city.

"What did I see?" he asked aloud, and he heard a laugh.

"You saw a bird," said a man, "for there was nothing else to see."

The man was walking along the roadway with a stick in his hand, and his eyes were bitter and mocking. "You are not a believer, I see," the man said.

"I am not. But neither am I an unbeliever." The Doubtful stood up, brushing the dust of the road off his clothes as well as he could.

"Allow me to guess," said the man. "They cast you out, because you would not worship their ridiculous god."

"I never found their god ridiculous," said the Doubter. "I found him terrible beyond all hope. What god could be so ruthless as to demand goodness of men?"

The passerby laughed. "That is droll, I'll admit. But this goodness they ask of you is as meaningless as their god. You need not cling to these shadows and dreams. Accept the reality of what is in front of you, and seek no other."

"Yet I doubt that too. You ask me to trust my eyes and not their dreams. I know no cause for trusting either."

"Then you are far more lost than I. One must know where to stop doubting."

"I don't think I believe that," said the Doubter, and the other man shook his head and walked away.

"The trouble is not that you couldn't see," said another voice, "but that you couldn't play with the things you saw. Don't you have any dreams of your own?"

The Doubter looked in every direction, but all he saw was the crow, perching nearby on the branch of a silver birch tree.

"I must have dreams of my own," he replied at last, "to be hearing you speak."

Then the crow on the branch stepped out of his crow skin and revealed himself as the magician called the Three Times Exiled. He grinned a grin from the branches of the tree, and the Doubter grinned back although he did not know why.

"Where are you from?" he asked. "For you are no mortal man."

The magician bowed, and said these words:

I've lived here on the borders of the night,
Where dark divides from light.
I've walked the marches made of fire and snow.

"I am only a visitor from the Country of the King, where no one believes anything, but everything is real. You may join me there if you like." And then he sang this song:

There are palaces and temples
In the cities on the plain
Made of bone as smooth as marble
Where the windows run like rain.

There's a grove of golden peaches,
There are apples, green and red,
There's a hierophant who teaches
From the gospels of the dead.

There are kings and queens, created
To be gods before the Fall-
Though you wandered there for ages
You could never see it all.

And your anguished hope of heaven,
Once a parched and withered thing,
Will be branches red with berries
In the country of the king.

"Why should I believe that?" asked the Doubter.

"You should not."

The Three Times Exiled jumped down from the branch, and the ground where he landed sprouted bells on stems, waving like flowers in a summer breeze. The sound of music filled the air

"Neither believers nor unbelievers will ever find it. I don't ask you to trust what others see or claim to have seen. I don't even ask you to trust what you see yourself. I ask you only to play."

The Three Times Exiled waved his hand, and a light burst forth from the Doubter's forehead and swept the world like a cloth washing paint away. The landscape around them became a world of wonder. But it was not exactly as the magician had described. Instead of a city made of bone there was a plain of windows, scattered here and there for hundreds of miles. Some of them were set into the ground and some rose up straight out of it; some of them floated in the sky and some moved from place to place. And every window looked out upon a different world, some of them fiery places and some of them snowy, some of them mountains and forests, others temples and palaces. The possibilities were so amazing that the Doubter merely gaped and did not even notice that the magician had gone.

"This is different than what you sang of..." he began, but then he saw he was alone. For only a moment, he stood dismayed. Then he walked off into the World of Windows and was seen no more.

Lore of Onei

The door to Sana Delayo is always open.

The Blue Pearl: a blue pearl of spiraling energy, capable of dissolving or transmuting any demonic power. Roll it in your hands to dissolve a nightmare.

The City: a magical city ruled by the Red Queen. The scene of many otherworld wars.

The Compass: an oracle owned by a king of Onei who was an ally of the Red Queen during the War of the Book. It is an old compass on a shipwreck mounted on a magnetic stone. It always predicts evil, and it makes sure that its own prophecies come to pass.

The Dark Tower: a gnostic prison where the Red Queen was once held prisoner. If you ever find it, you will discover that you have always been there. The bottom floor of the Dark Tower contains everything in mundane life, but merely spending time there causes you to forget where you really are. To escape the prison, do not run from wind or water. Allow the storm to destroy your dream.

Gnosis: true and sacred knowledge acquired from Onei.

The House: a vast, rambling house with countless rooms. Often attacked by malevolent forces. The attic is haunted.

The Kind: the fairies or elves. The folk of Onei.

The Naught: the other side of dream and death, a limitless soaring bliss or light. The Void. The divine darkness.

The Mysterium: magical power, a current of electricity or intoxication. It spins or spirals, either clockwise or counter-clockwise. It can be dark or light. It can dissolve loops and knots and destroy nightmares. It can possess you, either in Onei or the waking world. It can destroy the world and break through to the other side. It can appear as rising floodwaters, tsunamis, tornadoes, waterspouts or in other symbolic and ter-rifying forms. The mysterium can destroy all structure, all order. When the true power of the mysterium is unleashed, it can an-nihilate anything and everything, revealing the Naught.

Night Wandering: oneiromancy, the art of mythic dreaming.

Onei: the dream realm. It sends its messages by chance, yet it can be courted in trance. If you want knowledge, seek out darkness and silence.

A Power: a significant entity in Onei, such as a god, saint, angel or demon.

The Prime: warriors of the Kind. A regiment in the Red Queen's armies. The Prime has an initiation test consisting of strange riddles. If you answer perfectly, you pass. If your an-swers are almost correct, you fail. If your answers are com-pletely incorrect, you have a second chance to pass by going on a quest.

Sana Delayo: another word for Onei.

The Secret Library: a library on the rim of the Valley of Shadow, containing books on any and every topic from multi-ple different realities. The keepers of the library were cruel men, torturers and slavers, but the slaves rebelled and killed them, then disposed of their bodies in a lake. Not all of the masters were killed in the battle, and the survivors later counterattacked. The fate of the Secret Library remains uncertain. Later glimpses suggest that at least some grim powers may still be present there.

The Valley of Shadow: an infinitely deep valley of total darkness into which the dead must walk, led by a faceless guide with the mannerisms of a carnival barker. Many are too terrified to step down into the darkness, so they wander along the rim of the valley, angry and confused. If you go down into the darkness you can break through to the other side. The Valley of Shadow is the womb of the Naught.

Dream Quest: A journey or quest that occurs within a dream or series of dreams, for the purpose of achieving some mythic task or acquiring gnosis.

Answer all riddles; complete all quests.

"Don't Question Heaven"

I glance behind me, but there's no way home.
The waves are foaming like a rabid dog,
Like monsters, always watching. On my bones,
On every branch and rock and fallen log,
The ice lies thick. The silent heavens sleep-
Unreadable, malicious. Earth is still.
She won't disclose the secrets that she keeps.
Night creeps a little closer. From the hill
I hear the howl of wolves. I feel the eyes
Of basilisks upon me. Lions roar.
Don't question heaven. Do not leave your door.

Darkness and Silence

If you want knowledge, seek out darkness and silence. Dream necromancy is dangerous, especially if the spirit discovers your secret name.

Animal masking allows you to contact the cthonic powers.

To honor the gods, fumigate small images of them by hand in a cloud of incense.

The gods crave meat; the meat craves fire.

There are two types of death in dream. The dead force is like a black hole - without consciousness, dead and soulless although capable of movement. The live force is the exact opposite.

The universe is like the desert: a vast empty space made up of tiny particles lit by a blazing light.

There is no final invitation to Onei. You must find your way each time.

The pattern will always assert its essential points. Only a certain level of play exists in reality, and that which is destined cannot be prevented.

Some genii loci will abandon their home if it is clear-cut or otherwise abused. It becomes a soulless place.

There are time travelers who visit different eras by possessing dreamers as they sleep. If they come upon you in a night wandering dream they will try to stop your throat so you cannot get the words out, but if you force the words out you should be able to say your protective charm.

The whole world is filled up with gnosis. It is people who must become free in order to fill up gnosis.

The Country of the King

When your faith descends from heaven
When you find you cannot fly
When you lose the strength to bargain
With the powers of the sky,

When the things they keep demanding
Seem impossible and grand
You can come into the country
Of the powers of the land.

They have drunk from deeper waters
And their holiness is dark.
And to them the light is precious,
So they value every spark.

They are not inclined to question
What you've done or where you've been—
Though you've wandered far from wisdom
You can always come again.

There is gold beneath the mountain
There is treasure in the sea,
There's a chalice and a fountain
Granting things that cannot be.

There are palaces and temples
In the cities on the plain
Made of bone as smooth as marble
Where the windows run like rain.

There's a grove of golden peaches,
There are apples, green and red,
There's a hierophant who teaches
From the gospels of the dead.

There are kings and queens, created
To be gods before the Fall-
Though you wandered there for ages
You could never see it all.

And your anguished hope of heaven,
Once a parched and withered thing,
Will be branches red with berries
In the country of the king.

Under the Bright Dark

Do not hold on to that which cannot be used to destroy the world.
—The Livik

I was under the dark when the wind came down,
And the stars were drunk, and the ocean cried.
I walked alone. Though I had known
In time, I hadn't tried.

The world, disordered, spun as fast
As if it meant to break.
I liked it there, and didn't care
To suffer for its sake.

I've lived for years just mesmerized
By lights, like falling stars.
Out here beyond the world, I've watched
The angels and their wars.

I said the words that seemed the best
And watched my temples fall.
Those other lives I could have lived
Just don't exist at all.

The Ship of Stars

A flying ship gliding over an icy landscape.
You can use it to travel through Onei.

I walked across a plain of arctic ice
Beneath a sky of sharp and broken stars.
The world was flat and white, but shadowed scars

Lurked here and there across the frozen sea.
My heart was quiet, though the rising wind
Was howling like the devil's pipes. My skin

Was burning, faintly. Out there, in the night,
I saw the Ship of Stars against the snow.
Her boards were creaking, and an eerie glow

Clung, soft as mist, to ropes and flapping sails.
I climbed aboard and stood before the wheel
And with a sound of steel on sharpened steel

Her prow jumped out across the plain of ice.
The fog came in, and with it came a thought-
"Tonight's a night for flying." What I sought
Could lie in wait across this winter waste.

The Ship of Stars rose up into the night
And floated through the fog. Our only light

Came dimly through the wall of mist- a glow
From somewhere far away. My restless will
Grew vast, expansive, but as calm and still

As all the leagues of sky through which we flew.
I felt as insubstantial as a ghost.
"It won't be long," I thought. "I'm getting close."

A Journey to Onei (3)

The Book of Onei is not The Book," my father once said. I remember him still, walking beside me on that sunless beach – but was it before he had died, or after? "The Book of Onei is only a guide, a book of riddles that don't always lead to any answers, a book of truths within lies. I have been to Onei many times, but I have never been to any of the cities or nations mentioned in the Book of Onei, nor have I seen their ruins, nor met their citizens. As far as I can tell they do not exist, and most likely they never existed – not even in Onei."

"Then what is the Book of Onei?" I asked him. "Is it just a fraud?"

"The Book of Onei is both a key and a lock," he said. His face was haunted, as if he always listened and always waited – perhaps for a footfall. "Those stories mean something, but I do not know what. The Book of Onei hints at something, but I am afraid to ask."

"Perhaps all this darkness is just a means," I said, and yet he would not hear me and would not answer.

"So what is The Book, then?" I asked him.

"It contains all knowledge, all knowledge on any topic. It contains the secrets of the Primal Darkness! It is the gift of the Veiled One, the most ancient of all the Powers in Onei."

"Did she give it to you?"

"And why would she have done that? I snuck in to the library, the Great Library of Onei, and I stole what I wanted. I walked out with the Book of Onei in my coat pocket! What power would give me any aid or comfort?"

"Maybe that isn't something she would even care about. We know nothing about her. Perhaps the Book of Onei means nothing to her. Perhaps she wanted you to have it. Perhaps if you had ever made use of it, she would have shown you The Book. The real Book."

Still he did not answer, would never answer. He only looked at the ocean, at the light that flickered across the dark waters, and recited a poem:

"I'm Prometheus," he told me,
"I'm the traitor and the thief.
But his eyes were still defiant
Through his horror and his grief.

Then the eagle stuck its beak in
For the hundred millionth time,
And I watched in guilty wonder.
Was I worthy of his crime?

Have I used the gift he gave me?
Have I kept the embers warm?
Have I fed the god inside me
Striving daily to be born?"

And now here I stood, deep beyond the Borders of Onei, among the gorges and mountains. How far would I travel, how many mountains would I have to cross, until I discovered the secret? Was there even a secret to be uncovered, or only lies within lies?

I dug into my bag and found the Book of Onei, opened it up to a random page and read a poem about these mountains.

The Powers of Onei

The powers of Onei are infinite in number. To receive guidance from one of these powers, visualize the entity every night until you receive an answer—but be careful who you ask.

The Man Who Learned to Love the Law

I closed my eyes on all I saw.
And when I opened them, I'd learned to love the Law.
I found the garden where the shadows grew,
And look, I brought some home for you.

I closed my mouth on all I'd said.
I traveled west and south, and glorified the dead,
To taste their waters and to know if they were mine,
Or something else I'd lose in time.

I took my hand from all I'd held,
And offered recompense to dreams that I had felled.
They said I bore no guilt at all,
But still they'll watch me when I fall.

I closed my ears on all I'd heard.
The things I'd loved the most all died with just a word.
I kept them close to me for years,
Till they could be reborn as fears.

I took my mind from every scent
And none could ever find the places that I went.
The place in Avalon where Mordred grew.
And there was something there for you.
I've brought a chalice made of things I'd set aside.

I'll share this cup with you, and you can be my bride.
We'll drink the thunder and we'll ride the rising night,
And you can help me learn to love the light.

The Veiled One

The Veiled One is an ancient and terrifying old woman, "veiled" in the sense that her facial features cannot be clearly seen. In this, she is like one of the Legion, the Archons who control the world through the control of dreams.

She is the keeper of the Book, and she bestows it upon whomever she chooses. She can also teach many secret skills, but all of her wisdom is dangerous in one way or another. She stirs a whirlpool or cauldron made of swirling stars and galaxies. There is a black hole at the center of it.

You're going down into Death, down into the power that made Time!

I myself am afraid of it.

Boneyard Goddess

Burn a black candle and visualize the long-haired goddess of the graveyard, she who crouches on a tomb with her face in shadow. Recite this charm to dream of the dead.

Goddess of the boneyard, hear me
Through these ghosts that hover near me.
Clear the way through clay and water,
Death's companion, wisdom's daughter,
Clear the way that I may travel
Through this sand and rock and gravel,
Through this soil as black as midnight
To the place that knows no sunlight,
Only starshine always gleaming,
To the dead where they lie dreaming,
Bound by death's white silken tether.
They and I have work together.

Thou and I have work together!

Death Barker

A faceless guide who leads the dead into the Valley of Shadow. He doesn't speak, but only gestures grandly like a carnival barker for you to step down into the darkness. Nothing about him suggests that you should trust him.

No fear-
the slopes of death lead down
to utter darkness, and the clown
is faceless like the grave.
No fear-
the fear is everywhere
it's in the rocks, it's in the air.
He only grins and waves.
No fear-
the dead all weep and moan.
All love is lost, all life, all home.
The valley is so grim.
No fear-
and yet they're all afraid.
They cannot die, and so, dismayed
they wander on the rim.

The Host

The dreadful, eerie dead.

Those who would not or could not walk down into the Valley of Shadow.

Dead children gather at the quarters
And just stare at my house in silence,
As if the violence of their passing
Had wiped out all speech. Each of them has
Already attained the alien
Soulless quality of the angry dead.
I jump out of my bed and drive them
Off of my lawn. But there is no peace.
I didn't release them from what they
Suffered, and so they cannot move on.
In the quiet hours before dawn
The dead gather again with mindless
Grins. Vampire spirits, sharply-dressed,
Their eyes express a strange weightlessness.
But the pearl of alchemy is in
My hands. And though they perceive my plans,
They don't attempt to run. I transform
The dead dreams, and all the dead are gone.

The Blood Wisdom

A queen hanging from an apple tree on a plain of ice.

An apple tree upon a plain of ice,
Stands out against the sky. There hangs a queen,
Unclothed, but armed, among the leaves. Unseen,

The wheels of heaven turn. I feel their weight,
And in the cold I cannot catch my breath.
She grins at me. "It smells of sweat and death.

Blood wisdom's always like that. If you took
A cup of it you'd see it's dark as wine
And never sweet, but oh so strong. You'd find

Yourself upon an apple tree…" She laughs
And thunder rolls as if a mighty door
Had turned upon its hinge. "We've met before,"

That's all that I can say. She starts to keen,
A supersonic whine, as sharp and clear
As broken church bells. "Come and find me here."

This is the blood wisdom, and it smells of sweat and death.

The Red Queen

A pale, dark-haired fairy queen dressed in red. The Red Queen presides over the wild celebrations of the Kind.

The elven queen's in red tonight,
The night is hard and wild.
Her eyes reflect a distant light,
It makes him glad to see the sight.
He giggles like a child.

"I warned you once, each seven years…"
She says. Her face is grim.
The kiss she gave him long ago
Means little now, but even so,
It matters most to him.

"I kissed you once. It seemed that we…
But then, you had such words."
She cannot shake his foolish grin
Despite her people, closing in,
As close as hungry birds.

"I'm sorry that we ever met."
She says it soft and low.
They say the Lady has no heart.
That's true enough, but it was art
That snared her, even so.

"I always try to stop myself.
It always ends the same.
And you, so fair and full of flesh-
But it was I who wove the mesh."
She looks away in shame.

"Enough of this. The land of dreams
Demands your mortal life."
She lifts her hand and lets it fall-
And with a sudden, hungry call
She turns and draws the knife.

The Secret of Solomon

A mighty and terrifying dragon or traveler between worlds who can change shape and appear as male or female, dragon or human, or even as a pile of books. A powerful teacher of dream alchemy.

She looked at me— I call it she, although
No hint of human life was in its eyes—
And said, "I know you're scared, but do not rise.

"You've used the secret fire, but there is more.
We wish you to evolve." Her watchful face
Was wax-like, alien. I saw the place

She'd traveled from, and it was far- so far.
My chest was aching with a fear so cold
My blood felt sluggish. I had walked the old

And near-forgotten pathways. I had seen
My glimpse of burning wheels and turning gears,
And yet this creature woke my deepest fears

As easily as if she'd read the book
I keep sequestered in my hidden heart.
And yet, if she could teach the ancient art

Of changing roses into flying birds
And dreams to facts, and facts to other dreams-
I nodded slowly, and her cold eyes gleamed.

The Wonder, the Horror and the Art

A trio of goddesses named the Playful One, the Flowing One and Bloody-Face. The Playful One plays a bone harp. The Flowing One sings. Bloody-Face moans eerily in the form of a gray standing stone. The Flowing One once slew a dragon by diving into its mouth and cutting her way back out through its belly with her sword. Bloody-Face sometimes takes the form of a giantess dancing wildly, holding a severed head. The Playful One sometimes manifests as a little girl with curly hair, wearing a red dress. She can destroy worlds with the smallest gesture.

The three goddesses, when they were girls,
Were always quarreling. Bloody-Face
Would make a mess when the Flowing One
Sought to impress her friends. She would turn
Into a giantess and dance like
A madwoman with a severed head.
Meanwhile the Playful One, who was dressed
In red, didn't think it was funny
At all. And with a shake of her curls
She would destroy whole worlds. Now, these girls
Are all grown. Bloody-Face, made of stone,
Moans crazily in the winter wind.
The Playful One plays along on a

White harp made of bone. The Flowing One
Sings a song. They never got along.
And now, by the will of the great gods,
These three goddesses can never part.
The wonder, the horror and the art.

The Majesty

When the Majesty asked why the stars were put out, the Son of the First Man replied: "How could I know, with their begging and their radiance?"

Though he brought to the sun to the heavens,
Though he fished us out of a cold, cold star
Though he bound the worm to the waters
In a secret war.

Though he split the land from the water,
Though he put each star in its own true place
Though he spared us all from the slaughter
I fear his face.

He is a fiery dark god bursting free in destruction, a demiurge, a hunter of those who steal the fire of heaven. The least of his descendants are among the highest of the high.

I bent my knee once
And came down out of the majesty of death
Because I needed to learn to love the animal.
I desired to know myself in the anguish of multiplicity.

In my breathing out and my breathing in
In the birth and death of suns and planets
In my incarnation and my crucifixion.

In the city of ghosts where God walks, wreathed in fire.

The False Prophet

Although he has seen the truth, he spreads lies.

Clear water from a sacred stream
Has sanctified your vow,
But you remind me of a dream
That none remembers now.

You took a year I'd made of loss
And healed it in a day.
But that, I knew, would bear a cost
I wouldn't care to pay.

Now none remembers what you said,
The grief upon your brow.
You told us all to worship dread-
And who remembers now?

The Caesar Stones

The eyeless hermit waits in the desert and tends the Caesar Stones. You may appeal to them for guidance.

I've walked across this desert now for days.
The eyeless hermit waits beside the lake
Without a drop to soothe a pilgrim's ache.

The young girl asks me if I want to speak,
And I approach him, though my tongue feels thick.
He has no words. His teeth just hiss and click.

The Caesar Stones reveal themselves. A voice
Calls out across the salt flats: "Find me here."
The hermit laughs. The maiden starts in fear.

Powers Glimpsed in Onei

The powers of Onei are infinite in number. To receive guidance from one of these powers, visualize the entity every night until you receive an answer - but be careful who you ask.

The Red Boar: a mother boar fiercely defending her baby while a man kneels on the ground nearby and dips her Blood Spear into a well filled with all the blood shed on Earth. Take it directly from the fountain of dreams, and not from the dragon gate inscriptions.

The Acolyte: an angel weeping in a crypt, imprisoned for bearing corrupted scriptures or forbidden knowledge to earth. Is this the only reason to fall? Or to slay or be slain? I corrupted my message with lies, causing the sons of mirth to sing false songs to the listening lords.

The Bloodstone: a megalithic altar of blood sacrifice beside the ocean. The world was made from the blood of sacrifice.

The Exiles: exiled aristocrats begging for food and drink. There was an unpleasant side to the faces of the gods. They melted like butter.

The Haunting: an invisible but horrifying presence. The silent emptiness of the lonely places, the awful quietness of a locked room.

The Keeper of Dust: an aged librarian whose books are fading and crumbling into dust. All works must fade. Not even in the most subtle sense will they survive.

The Leviathan: a great whale with a staring eye. A massive, marked-out whale, a rebel against the Law.

The Lion's Mouth: a fierce king who threatens death and horror unless you do evil on his behalf. To fear the evil and to love the good, and so do evil thereby, or to fear no evil and love no good and so remain unstained.

The Livik: an old mystic who found a number code in an old book, the solution of which is a blank page. Do not hold on to that which cannot be used to destroy the world.

Lord One-Eye: the ruler of Castle One-Eye and keeper of the Oliac Axis, a key that allows access to any level of Faery. Lord One-Eye is a bedridden but dangerous old vampire. He commands an army of automata. The Dreamer came and took the Oliac Axis from him while looking for the Red Queen. You must learn that you know nothing, to discover some strange, unpleasant thing.

The Shy Girl: a small girl who lives in a place haunted by a powerful ghost leader. You need to stop trying to understand. Sometimes a thing has five meanings, but grown-ups always want it to have one.

Wine into Water: a teacher who turns dark wine into holy water. Every speck in the city is a universe. There is no salvation, because there is nothing in you to save or be damned. There is only the infinite.

The Legion: The Archons who control the world through the control of dreams. The Lords of the Earth are cloaked in power; power keeps them warm.

The Beast: a monstrous demonic man, a cannibalistic killer and sorcerer. He serves the Shapeshifter.

The Falling Sun: an apocalyptic demonic god, a comet or fireball falling on a city. It seeks entrance to our world. The War of the Book was fought to keep it from gaining the power of the Book.

The Fell Sisters: triumphantly evil nuns with white eyes, marbleized faces, and long disheveled black hair. Members of the Legion.

The Ghost Leader: a member of the Legion. He haunts the mountains and offers initiation into his corrupt tradition.

Mr. Triumph: a seldom-seen but very dangerous sorcerer who lives in a remote house in the country with the evil toys he calls his "worms." A branch covered with red berries keeps him trapped, because he can't remove it himself.

The Seventh Man: an albino demon in purple robes, a servant of the Shapeshifter. He makes threats and offers bargains.

The Shapeshifter: a ferocious child-haunting goddess or queen of demons who can change into many terrifying shapes and forms. She mesmerizes victims with the power of her will, and she is great among the Legion.

When you meet a demon, dissolve yourself.

The Story of the Man Who Learned to Love the Law

There was a man in the Qalina who did not love the Law and complained of it bitterly to all who would listen. The Law of the Qalina was an unforgiving code, with numerous infractions both great and small. To complain of any of the provisions of the Law was held the same as to break them, so the man who did not love the law was shunned by all. Some of his neighbors even informed on him, and he was forced to flee from one place to another like a hunted animal.

He became accustomed to living in caves and the holes in trees, to the scent of roots and the flavor of earthworms. He learned to love silence and darkness. He learned the love of another Law.

One night he heard a voice and knew instantly that it was the voice of the Adoration, the terrible god of the Empire. What it said was this: "I bent my knee once and came down out of the Majesty of Death because I needed to learn to love the animal. I desired to know myself in the anguish of multiplicity."

He came out of the roots of a tree that night as the sun was setting, looked around in all directions, and smiled like a mask. He set out for the west, toward the primal waters, the chaos ocean from which the world was made. He wanted to drink a mouthful of the waters of the dead, to determine for himself if he had understood this revelation. Was the Law of the Roots and Caves a way and a prophecy, or only a delusion brought on by loss?

He traveled for many months, in silence and darkness, moving through deep forests in the dead of night. He was like a lone wolf on the edge of the campfires, eyes shining on the border of the light before disappearing into shadows. But however far to the west he traveled, he could find no chaos ocean. Had the priests of the Adoration merely lied? Was there even such a thing as the primal waters?

He turned south then, in response to a rumor. The people to the west of the empire said that the chaos ocean was in the distant south, and he hoped and wondered although he could not be certain. He praised the dead in his nightly prayers, because the Law of the Roots and Caves is the wisdom of the dead and teaches the Majesty of Death from which the Adoration arose. He dwelt in the drunken unconsciousness of the void between the stars.

And the anguish of multiplicity was all around him, the Adoration broken into shards of consciousness like splinters of glass, learning slowly to know itself, mired in the cruelties of its own creation. He understood evil then, as the priests did not. The Adoration was imperfect. The Adoration was lost, a broken mind in many pieces. How could there possibly not be evil? In every self in which it manifested, in every pair of eyes through which it saw, the Adoration was learning. And those who are learning must make mistakes. On the peak of a desolate mountain he knelt down to pray, then turned again in silence and darkness.

Yet there was no chaos ocean in the deepest south. The man who had learned to love the Law was confused and lost, as lost as the god he had discovered how to love. He began to despair, and a wildness entered into his prayers for the dead. How could there be no chaos ocean, however far he wandered? How could there be no primal waters?

There was a woman in his home city—not a true city, for there were few of those, but one of the ruined cities of the wasteland where small clusters of people still huddled among the shells of once-great structures—and he had loved her once, as well as he could. Love does not come easily to the deeply wronged. He thought of her now in his despair and his loneliness, and he yearned to return to her and see her face again. He wanted her to teach him something, to give him something he thought she had, though it was only his own yearning he chose to see in her. He appeared in her window one night like a haunting revenant, and as she shrank back into her bedsheets he spoke these words:

> *I closed my eyes on all I saw.*
> *And when I opened them, I'd learned to love the Law.*
> *I found the garden where the shadows grew,*
> *And look, I brought some home for you.*

She backed away from him in horror and dread, knowing that the Law he loved was not the Law of the Qalina, but some more ancient and darker code. Had he truly visited the primal waters, had he walked in the Garden of Shadows, could he drink the thunder and ride the night? She did not know. All she knew was this.

Neither she nor anyone else would ever teach him to love the light.

In the twisted roots beneath a pale old tree beneath the windows of the woman he loved, the man who had learned to love the law met a serpent in the shadows. The serpent reared up to him and swayed back and forth, and its eyes were like black pebbles. The man was not frightened although the serpent was venomous. He only sighed and expressed regret. "If I had stayed at home," he said. "If I had remained silent..."

And the serpent replied:

I've been looking into
The crevices between moments
For so many years now
That I could tell you their species:
Some of them look like
Fossilized sea creatures
With spiral anatomies
And some look like the scales
On the wings of dragonflies.
There are some that look
Like the colors in
A cat's eyes
When it thinks no one is looking,
And there are some
Like potentialities.

I picked up a lacuna
In my own memories
And tried to taste it once,
But it turned out
To be poisonous.
"Might have beens" are that dangerous.

He looked at the serpent and he understood. The primal waters are not found so easily, and the Chaos Ocean is not a place you can walk to. The black depths from which the Adoration arose are in the crevices between moments, buried deeper than the deepest roots, further underground than the darkest cave. The Law of the Roots and Caves is to keep on burrowing, to dig deeper and ever deeper. Once the path has been decided upon, there is no return. To wish for things that might have been is to lose the way.

A Journey to Onei (4)

When my father told me about the Lords of the Earth, I was riding a bus along a lonely highway. No head-lights passed us, and no stars shone. The sun had long set and was far from rising. This was after my father's death but before the birth of my own child. I was in trouble with the law at that time, as I have often been.

I couldn't sleep, but something shimmered in the window in front of me like a reflected dream. It was the ghost of my fa-ther – fainter this time, deader this time. I picked up our con-versation where we'd left off, eager despite my own troubles to learn more of Onei.

"Are the Powers gods?" I asked him. He nodded silently, as if he respected my refusal to speak of anything personal. The dead have other concerns.

"A god is a certain type of Power, but not all Powers are gods. Some are heroes, and some are saints, some are ghosts and some are devils. The Powers of Onei are infinite in num-ber. To hear the words of such a Power, you need only hold the entity in your mind each night until you receive an answer in your dreams - but be careful who you ask for such a favor. The most terrible by far are the Lords of the Earth."

"And who are the Lords of the Earth?"

"The tyrants of dream. Rulers of what we can imagine, they rule the world. You won't find them any safer to defy than these earthly powers you have so offended. Remember, son – most of what you will read in the Book of Onei does not exist at all. The secret is clothed in shadows; it wears lies like a veil."

And yet I had crossed the Starry River and read the future in its constellations. I had crossed the Plain of Night on foot and heard the whispers, the dread conspiracies. I had gazed on the ruins of the City of Wisdom and laughed along with the birds who nest there. No one had ever thought to rebuild that place after the Sons of the Crow came down on Onei. No one ever will.

Now I stood here before the City of the Gods in the Plain of Day, one of the nations my father had assured me had never existed—not even in dream.

But had it existed before I came there?

No map of Onei is ever complete, nor even particularly useful.

Except the one you draw yourself.

Exorcism

The Three Types of Nightmare

Nightmares can possess other dream entities, places in Onei and places or people in the waking world. Dream exorcism is the art of dissolving nightmares.

Broadly speaking, there are three types of nightmares.

Night hunters are dream assassins. Revenants are of the Host, the dreadful dead. Legionaries are demonic gods, great but terrible powers of Onei.

You can fight any nightmare if you need to, but if you are wounded it may be able to possess you through your dream, controlling your body when you wake up. It is wise to have a protective charm committed thoroughly to memory, so you can recite it even in your sleep if you need to. You can break any enchantment or banish any dream with a sufficiently powerful charm, but to prevent this a nightmare may try to stop up your mouth so you can't say the words. Keep struggling until you can say them.

The nightmares may threaten you, offer to initiate you or try to make a Faustian bargain with you. Great discernment is needed in these cases, because some entities are legitimate teachers or initiators even if terrifying, while others only cor-rupt. Hostile spirits can become allies or spirit teachers if you make the right kind of peace with them.

The Blue Pearl Charm

To disperse or dissolve a malign spirit, raise the mysterium in the form of a ball of energy, sometimes known as the blue pearl. Play with the blue pearl until the knot unties and the nightmare is dissolved. The spirit may try to fight you for control of the power so it can gain possession. Never take this work lightly, as it is far from safe.

I place the blue pearl of the dragon kings into my own chest in place of my heart. My light shines out over the four worlds!

The nature of this art is to remove all hindrance. Information flows freely in its natural state. It only goes into a loop and repeats the same song over and over when something has gone wrong.

And the worst of these loops are the lords of the earth—information vampires and black holes, all of them. Is there any worth in becoming a kind of tar-pit of the infinite?

To attain such weight that none of the facts of which you are composed is in its natural state, but all of them trapped and frozen, with the mark of the dead- that sense that there is no person within you, and that alien dread?

Well, I am here to exorcise you, and make no mistake—the blue pearl of the worms of heaven is both my cross and my stake.

Send the Dead to the Dead

Not all the dead are the same. Some want peace, and some want vengeance, some to complete a task and some to right a wrong. The dead can be enemies and the dead can be allies. The dead can need help and the dead can give help. Never assume.

A revenant needs to be exorcised if it is causing harm, if it feeds on the blood of the living or if it asks for release.

To exorcise the malign dead by sending them back where they belong, roll the blue pearl against the sun. Recite these words: "Send the dead to the dead."

Send the dead to the dead,
To the dead they go.
To the water and clay
Of the world below.
To the flickering torches
And silent halls.
To the stone and the bone
And the dark, wet walls.

Send the dead to the dead,
With the dead they sleep.
With the worms and the roots
And the things that creep.

Let them rot and decay
In their narrow rooms
Till the dawn of the day
When the graveyard blooms.

Vampires

If the dead come knocking, don't let them in unless you know they mean no harm to you or yours. They may want to attach themselves to you, draining your blood through your dreams.

The tiger paces—muscle, fur and bone.
His eyes are flat and crazy- from his breath
Rolls out a stench of rotting flesh. My death

Has come to find me, and my heart descends
Through nearly forty years. I scream and scream
"Oh no, oh no, please daddy, stop this dream."

I hear a voice: "You cannot run or hide,
Or clothe yourself in harness. What we show
Will weigh on you and trip you up. To know

The mystery of life and death is such
As few would bear." I nod my dull assent.
And violently, perceiving my intent,

The whole world changes. While I sit to write
Before my cluttered desk, a man arrives
To tell me that my own sweet daughter dies

*Of some most painful cancer. And I cry
"I love you, oh I love you." And she screams,
"Oh no, oh no, please daddy, stop this dream."*

Transformation of Spirits

Dissolving spirits is dream exorcism. No spirit can be dissolved forever; it will always return with the conditions that gave rise to it.

Transformation of spirits is dream alchemy, and much more difficult than dream exorcism. To transform a spirit, raise the mysterium with a mentality of nonduality and nonresistance. If you can do this successfully, the spirit will transform right in front of you into a human being or a creature of light or whatever else it needs to be.

Between the cold gray stones of the old
Barrow, I feel its fear. A strange wight
Is coming near. A being so potent
It can burst the bonds and pull it out
Of its long sleep to a dark so deep
It would lose its dreaming. With a shout
I cast out that wight, and with my hands
I unweave the bands of the barrow's seeming
So it can die in its own dreaming.

Power of Powers

Oh I am the wings with which I fly
And I am the wind, and I am the sky.
And I am the sun of the city of light,
And I am the star, and I am the night.
And I am the snake in her mountain home,
And I am the mother's mournful moan.

No harm can nightmare do to me:
Power of powers I have on thee.

And I am the dawn, and I am the flame,
And I am the word and the song and the name,
And I am the red of the leaping spark,
And I am the blaze that flashed in the dark -
That lit the dark and made the sun,
And stars like candles, one by one.

No harm can nightmare do to me:
Power of powers I have on thee.

Oh I am the smith and the hammer too
And the note of the anvil so clear and true.
And I am the singer, and I am the song
That praised the right, that shamed the wrong.
And I am the healer whose caring hand

Can crack the ice and wake the land.
And I am the sky, so bright and true,
And you're in me, and I'm in you.

No harm can nightmare do to me:
Power of powers I have on thee.

Poppet-Binding Exorcism

1: Gather several responsible and careful helpers who will neither panic nor go to excesses, holy water of some kind, a poppet, a rope and a box covered with binding and warding figures.

2: During the waning moon, place the poppet on the subject and bless the subject with holy water, fumigation, prayers and so forth until the entity flees into the poppet. Use "send the dead to the dead" if appropriate, or "Cast it out, drive it forth, let it flee from what's ours, in the name of the gods and the spirits and the powers."

3: Ritually bind the poppet and place it in the box, then ritually bind and safely dispose of the box. Great care must be taken at every stage. This operation can take one to several days.

The Gift of Horror

A nightmare is a precious opportunity, the gift of horror. This is the secret of the darkseers: to transform horror into wonder, to raise vast power through awe and terror, to use that power to destroy the dream structure. The bliss on the other side is beyond conception.

The crystal darkness broke apart,
I watched the pieces fall.
To find and fix them takes an art
I don't possess at all.

It comes to this- we'll have to live
Without them for a while.
In love with horror, courting things
That laugh but never smile.

We come to you with broken beaks
And wings like crippled birds.
It's better not to even speak
Than lose the weight of words.

A Journey to Onei (5)

The night hunters found me in the land beyond the forest, where I had thought to camp for the night to escape the rigors of the journey. My preparations had been extensive, including offerings and fumigations, and yet they slipped in past my wards regardless. There is no certainty in war.

I was on a vast and treeless plain, a place of dead grass and smoldering fires. Barrow mounds brooded between circles of stone, the tombs of dead gods and forgotten kings. The night was silent, as still as a hunted animal. The moon was dark.

I thought long on the past, brooding on friends lost and causes broken. Such thoughts are useless, yet they fill up the empty spaces like rushing waters. I thought of my wife and my dear daughter, a continent away from me now, and in another world. I thought of my father, the thief who had stolen this book. I thought of the Legion, the horrors that feed on horror. I thought of their promises and I thought of their threats.

I knew something they didn't know, but I did not yet know the secret.

"Darkseer, we have come for you," said a quiet voice. I looked out into the darkness past the campfire and saw the image of a man. His face was a smeared shadow, a hint of something unseen and un-seeable. He dangled something from his fingers… perhaps a watch. Or perhaps flesh. Twelve others exactly like him were closing in from all directions.

"And what have I done to offend you?" I asked sarcastically, knowing the answer as well as they did. My melancholy lifted. It has always been like this for me. Without a foe, I cannot thrive.

"That is long past mending," said the hunter. "If you had returned what you carry, if you had taken your own life in remorse… perhaps then we would have spared you. What your father did was unforgivable, but for you it is worse than that."

"You misunderstand the situation." I chuckled. "I am not here to pay my debt to Onei."

"Then why have you come at all?" the creature asked, as the twelve who followed him formed a circle. They intended to allow me no escape.

And I intended no escape.

"I came here to erase you," I said, and made the blue pearl between my hands.

The night hunters began to scream, but they were right the first time. It was long past mending.

Night Hunting and War Wizardry

Sons of the Crow

And are we not of the sons of the crow,
Who worship a hidden creed?
Or those who seek but do not know,
And hear, but do not heed?

And should I draw the sacred sword
And hold it in my hand,
To bring the fury of our Lord
Through this corrupted land?

Or should I cast the foolish night
Of vengeance to the sun?
Or should I face that deadly light
From which the angels run?

And are we not of the sons of the sky,
Who worship the hidden star?
Or those who neither live nor die
But watch it from afar?

Night Hunting

Night hunting is the art of waging war via night wandering dreams. You can defend yourself against such attacks using charms, dream alchemy, the war figures and other methods. Some night hunters are from the waking world and some from the dream world.

There are places in Onei that teach the art of night hunting, such as the War Wizard College. There are also dream traps that will trigger an enchantment if touched or approached.

The War Figures

A figure is a sigil. The War Wizard College teaches the use of the War Figures, of which the figure called Melting Hands is a most powerful ward. It prevents enemy enchantments from taking hold. Sleep with it under your pillow to protect against night hunters.

Never forget, war magic is violence.

Binding

This charm will bind a powerful enemy who stands in your way or oppresses you. Burn a black candle and bind a poppet in the form of your enemy with the hair from a dead man's head.

Shadows of the vale of horrors
Where all journeys end,
Drink this cup of blood and fire,
Know me as your friend.

Drink this clotted wine and gather.
There is one who stands,
Blocking all the paths before me.
Bind his upraised hands.

Seal his lips with locks of iron
Fill his limbs with lead.
Cross his eyes with letter Xs
Fill his dreams with dread.

Douse the stars that fill his heavens,
Break his brittle pride.
Leave him powerless and hopeless
Till he steps aside.

Antinomian

I climbed a staircase to the land of birds
And told them what I'd learned.
They didn't care.
To birds, the world is made of clouds and air.

I dove into the waters of the deep
And sang a poem to sharks.
They swam on by.
I might as well have sung of stars and sky.

I heard the demon's sermon, and his voice
Was sweet as thick molasses,
But his creed
Was not convenient to my present need.

So, if I haven't walked the darkest paths
Of which my kind is capable
The cause
Is not that I have dearly loved His laws.

Night Hunters

Redsheet: a nighthunter involved in the War of the Book. It initially appeared as a humanoid figure in a red sheet, then as a series of abstract shapes, then as an eel with poisonous amber blood, then as crocodilian monster, then as a monstrous, snapping machine.

The Gray Goblin: a nighthunter who eats eyes. Blinded in retribution during the War of the Book.

Mask Demons: nighthunters who served the Falling Sun during the War of the Book. The mask itself is a dangerous possessing spirit.

The Puritan: a killer who ruthlessly destroys the wicked.

Rampage: a murderer who paints bright, vibrant surrealist portraits of both his victims and their mourners. I'm not in heaven and I'm not in hell. It will give you the power of an animal, but it will kill you.

The Steam Machine: a hungry, threatening, steam-powered vehicle, brightly colored and covered with bellows and levers.

Mr. Flint: one of the Legion, a night hunter who appears as a faceless man in a dark suit.

Warding Spell

Burn a white candle and recite this charm to ward your space. At every corner of the compass, draw a protective figure with a stick of burning incense.

I ward the east with flame and water,
Sealing off this door.
I raise this pillar to the skies.
No ghost with evil in its eyes
Can enter anymore.

I ward the south with mirth and music,
Locking up this gate.
I raise this pillar to the south.
No revenant with grinning mouth
Can come here bearing hate.

I ward the west with smoke and spittle,
Blocking off the path.
I raise this pillar to ensure
No demon through the western door
Shall enter in its wrath.

I ward the north with blood and fire,
Closing up the walls.
I raise this pillar to the night.

No fearsome or unwholesome wight
Gains entrance to these halls.

I ward the four directions, praising
Death's dissolving grace.
I praise the pillars of the land,
The mighty dead who rise and stand
On guard around this place.

The Wild Hunt

An army of the dead rides the night sky on an endless hunt, chasing the souls of the damned across the heavens. To set the Hunt on the trail, soak a picture of the guilty party in the spit of a dog and bury it in a glass jar in the depths of the forest. Raise a cairn over the jar, and recite these words:

When my eyeballs bloom like flowers
And my hands go forth to war,
When the bell that tolls the hours
Cracks and falls and rings no more,

When the oceans turn to deserts
Made of salt as fine as sand
Will you still deny your treasures?
Will you stop and understand?

You can build a cage for tigers
And pretend that they are tame
You can serve the rage of liars
While you glorify the Name,

You can still the tongue that teaches,
You can kill the eyes that see,
And however far my reach is
You can still attempt to flee.

But the sum of all your errors
Will be reckoned in the score,
And you'll pay the price in terror
When my heart goes forth to war.

A Journey to Onei (6)

On the shores of the Chaos Ocean, by the Primal Darkness, I walked alone with a song on my lips. I had stood on this beach before; I knew that now. I had walked here with my father's ghost. He had recited a poem about Prometheus.

It was just as I had told my wife, so long ago. The secret of the Book of Onei is in the primal waters, in the heart of the Chaos Ocean. It is not a technique, and nor is it a thing that can be known. To find it out for yourself, you have to go there in person.

There was no sun in the heavens, and there were no stars either. There was only a light, flickering distantly as if from some lonely shore. That light had frightened my father, and he had glanced back at it often, seeming to keep it in mind as we talked. He must have expected it to call him back, though to what it called him I did not know. It frightened me now, but I had decided to welcome that fear. Horror is both a lock and a key, at least to a darkseer. I wondered if I would find him in the darkness, or if he would already have moved on.

I called to the Ship of Stars with her sign and her song, and waited in silence as the waves rolled in, crashing mindlessly on those empty shores. I waited for a day there, or I waited for a year. I waited for ten thousand years. It doesn't matter.

And then it was there at last, like a falling leaf, settling gently into the primal waters. Its white sail flapped, and the ship's wheel turned and creaked. I put my hand on the prow, stroking the wood like the head of a dog.

"Take me to that light," I said, and it shuddered in protest. The Ship of Stars is alive, as all dreams are alive. And what lives, knows fear.

"I know what the light is," I said. "I know where it leads. I need you to take me there."

The Chaos Ocean is terrible, the birthing place of all nightmares on earth. Of all that is. It swarms with monsters, though nothing swims in its lightless depths. It bubbles them up as if casting them out, but it can never be defined by any of them. I sailed those waters, crossing the gulfs between distant stars. The wind between the worlds is what drove me on, howling its lonely song. I searched for eons, but the light was always equally distant.

When the monsters came up at me, I did not destroy them. I no longer desired their fear, though I could dissolve them with the blue pearl. I no longer wanted to hear them scream. Instead I transformed them. I who was once an exorcist had become an alchemist, capable of changing demons to angels. The grasping arms and gaping jaws, the slick teeth wet with hunger – all this I changed, and the demons themselves were the first to thank me. They rose up from the husks of their bodies as burning wheels, as gears and eyes and wings.

The light came no closer.

Dream
Alchemy

The Fire and Water Scroll

The skill of fire is the ability to raise energy
The skill of water is the ability to direct energy
The skill of earth is the ability to dissolve energy
The skill of air is the ability to change energy
The skill of the void is the ability to transcend energy.

The power of fire and water is the foundation of the work
The power of earth and air is the work itself,
The power of the void is the work completed.

Whoever has the skill of fire is a novice
Whoever has the skill of water is a magician
Whoever has the skill of earth is an exorcist
Whoever has the skill of air is an alchemist
Whoever has the skill of the void is one of the makers of the
world.

The skill of fire before the skill of water
The skill of water before the skill of earth
The skill of earth before the skill of air
And the skill of air before the void.

The skill of fire is inspiration
The skill of water is art
The skill of earth is the exorcism of demonic forces

And the skill of air is their transformation.
The skill of the void is not a skill.

Whoever would begin must raise the secret fire
Whoever would continue must direct it
Whoever would purify it must still its passion
And add new fuel to it to change its light.
Whoever would transcend it must dissolve the dream.

The initiation of fire is when you learn to raise energy
The initiation of water is when you learn to play with it
The initiation of earth is when you can dissolve a demon to
untie a knot
The initiation of air is when you learn how to change it
The initiation of the void is when you become the golden
child.

The art of the fire includes all methods of raising energy
The art of the water, all methods of leading it
The art of the earth includes all methods of stilling energy,
And the art of the air includes all elixirs.
The art of the void is not an art.

Theory of Dream Alchemy

The waking world is made of dreams. Dream energy is the prima materia, the stuff of reality. The natural condition of dream is to flow and develop spontaneously and freely, but dream energy can become stuck or trapped. Recurring patterns in dream are common, but these patterns exist in a relationship with the total environment - they still develop and flow according to their own nature. Dream loops are different, because they can only repeat themselves and can never change.

When dream energy becomes looped and stagnant, the result is a haunting - a nightmare repeating the same patterns over and over, trapped in dreamspace with no ability to change or develop outside of the pattern. All people are haunted to one degree or another, enslaved by dream loops they cannot escape. Dream alchemy is the art of cutting these knots and loops, restoring the free and spontaneous flow of dream. The art of dream alchemy begins with exorcism, then moves beyond that to transformation, proceeding at last to annihilation.

The Language of the Birds

The moment you establish a relationship with an idea, it enters space-time and has a history. This is the only real language that has ever existed. Every dream has a story; to change the dream, change the story.

My heart and I were like a pair of crows
Beneath a quiet sky
Of evening snows.
I tried to sing aloud-
She laughed at me,
And said I was too proud
To ever see.
And though I've held the traces of the light,
I can't forget that night.

My heart and I were like a pair of birds
Of some forgotten kind
That once had words.
I turned and spoke her name.
She flew away,
With words of so much shame
I cannot say.
And though I've tasted seven kinds of fear
It seems I still can hear.

I left my heart at last and walked alone
Where worlds had never spun
Nor stars had shone.
I turned and fiercely cried
She came to me
When I had nearly died
Beside the sea.
She dove into my chest and beat at last.
I broke apart the past.

The Five Operations

The five basic alchemical operations are calcinatio, solutio, coagulatio, sublimatio and coniunctio. Each operation is performed on the prima materia or dream energy you want to work with - your own mind, a situation you are trying to change or a nightmare you meet in Onei.

First is calcinatio, or the fire operation. Raise the mysterium or secret fire, the raw energy of dream, also known as the blue pearl. Heat up the secret fire by playing with it and letting it move and flow through different patterns.

Second is solutio, or the water operation. Gently direct the mysterium through different changes. There is a clockwise spiral, a counterclockwise spiral, an infinity figure-eight, a feeling of expanding outwards, a feeling of contracting inward and a feeling of pushing straight forward. You may find the same patterns, or you may find others. Once you can feel how the energy wants to move in that moment, try to nudge it gently into other patterns. For instance, a clockwise spiral, if you make it tight enough, can suddenly reverse into a counterclockwise spiral, and vice versa. A figure-eight can become either spiral. The important thing is to never fight what the energy wants to do. Instead, ride the spiral until a point is reached where the energy could just as easily do one thing as another, and guide it at that moment into doing the one you have chosen. If you work on this for a while, your breathing should naturally become deep and regular, and the feeling of the secret fire should become more distinct and powerful.

Third is the coagulatio or earth operation. Allow the blue pearl to expand until it dissolves itself and all other dreams within its influence. You can use this to dissolve a nightmare or an enchantment, so the earth operation is dream exorcism.

Fourth is the sublimatio or air operation. Use the blue pearl to transform the dream, cutting any knots or loops and allowing the dream energy to flow freely and spontaneously into new shapes and forms. This is true dream alchemy, and much more difficult than dream exorcism.

Fifth is coniunctio, the operation of the void. When the mysterium rises in its most powerful form, it manifests in Onei as a storm or a flood, or any other terrifying and destructive power. You may want to run or fight. If you can remember to let it destroy you or to dissolve yourself instead of running or fighting, this mighty power will destroy the dream world. This is the annihilation.

Dream Elixirs

Another way to approach dream alchemy is through the use of an elixir. An elixir is any new information or power that can dissolve a loop and change a dream.

In dream itself, you may experience an elixir as a pill or a potion. However, an elixir can be a new course of action, a new way of thinking, a cup of tea, a glass of wine, a constellation or your imagination. To create an elixir, go into the Borderlands and imagine a set of symbolic elements corresponding to the quality you wish to introduce into your dreamspace. You can make an amulet, compose a poem, paint a painting or tell a mythic story with the desired symbolism embedded in it. Any method of introducing the intended ideas into your dreamspace can be effective.

Alchemical Correspondences

This is a simplified set of alchemical correspondences. Every symbol within a particular set can be used as a stand-in for any other symbol or concept in that set, even though each can be negative or positive or neutral depending on which quality is focused on. If one of the negative qualities is manifesting, it may indicate an imbalance of that energy:

Saturn: fire, lead, black, the crow, limitation, materialism, neurosis, stubbornness, prudence.

Jupiter: water, tin, white, the fish, emotions, nightmares, beauty, friends, excess.

Mars: air, iron, red, swords, assertiveness, wealth, courage, power, violence.

Venus: earth, copper, green, chains, love, pleasure, bliss, passion, sexuality.

Mercury: mercury, turquoise, grapes, consciousness, inspiration, transformation, intuition, speech, cleverness.

Moon: silver, white, chalices, magic, wisdom, knowledge, intuition, coolness, detachment.

Sun: salt, gold, purple, the eagle, vitality, enlightenment, success, illumination, arrogance.

Dream Talismans

1: choose a set of symbols to represent the situation you wish to change.

2: create a paper talisman using the symbols you selected.

3: burn the talisman down to ashes.

4: mix paint with the ashes using the symbolic color of the desired dream energy.

5: use the paint to create a new talisman with a new set of symbols representing the change you wish to create.

The Starry Powers

The starry powers may be invoked under the traditional Zodiac signs and symbols. Each of the seven starry powers has a gift to give, an elixir to be tasted and a price to be paid.

The Headless Immortal is an old sage who lives alone in the mountains. He can remove or attach his head at will. He gives the gift of fortitude and requires your own head as his price. He may be invoked under the sign of the Goat, with the words "To work harder and to do more, in a night cave throughout the night."

Wine into Water is an alchemist who specializes in turning dark red wine into holy water. He gives the gift of unearned liberation and requires only your hope of salvation as his price. He may be invoked under the sign of the Water Bearer, with the words "Every speck in the city is a universe. There is no salvation, because there is nothing in you to save or be damned. There is only the infinite."

The Bloodstone is a megalithic altar of blood sacrifice beside the ocean. It gives the gift of sacrifice, the power to do what must be done. The Bloodstone's gift is the same as its price. It may be invoked under the sign of the Fish, with the words "I came down out of the majesty of Death because I needed to learn to love the animal."

The Weaver is a small but reckless spider, weaving its web on your outstretched hand. It gives the gift of courage, and its price is the consequence of impulsive behavior. It may be invoked under the sign of the Ram, and it requires no words but only a decision.

The Fiery Bull is a giant fire-breathing bull-god holding a harp as he bursts into a fort. He gives the gift of practical hedonism and demands irrational stubbornness as his price. He may be invoked under the sign of the Bull and needs no words but only determination.

The Changeling is a fairy changeling, a counterfeit human with a massively swollen yet empty head. It gives the gift of imagination and flexibility, and the price it asks is an attitude of devious superficiality. It may be invoked under the sign of the Twins, with the words "They have a regular child with a regular body, so they think what they have is a human being."

The Red Boar is a mother boar fiercely defending her baby. She gives the gift of fierce loyalty. You can summon her under the sign of the Crab by kneeling and dipping her Blood Spear into a well filled with all the blood shed on Earth. You can also use the words "Take it directly from the fountain of dreams, and not from the dragon gate inscriptions."

The Sun King is an itinerant sword-master with the sun inside him. The beams are always escaping through his pores. He gives the gift of regal confidence and disdain but requires unreasonable flattery as his price. He may be invoked under the sign of the Lion with the words "Am I not dripping with gems like liquid?"

The Shy Girl is a little girl who lives in a place haunted by a powerful ghost leader. She gives the gift of creativity and all forms of success requiring cleverness. The price she requires is rank confusion. She may be invoked under the sign of the Virgin, with the words "You need to stop trying to understand. Sometimes a thing has five meanings, but grown-ups always want it to have one."

The Keeper of Injustice is a goddess holding a pair of scales. She gives the gift of diplomacy and the price she requires is that you answer her question. She may be invoked under the sign of the Scales, with the words "What gives the greatest happiness?"

The Blood Wisdom is a queen hanging from an apple tree on a plain of ice. She gives the gift of blood wisdom, and the price she requires is sweat and death. She may be invoked under the sign of the Scorpion, with the words "This is the blood wisdom, and it smells of sweat and death."

The Archer is a goddess on a bridge over a bay, sinking ships with arrows from her massive bow. She once carried another god on her boat to be healed by a wise man, but the wise man gave him to the people of earth, who ate him instead. She gives the gift of optimism, and a helpful sense of direction and purpose. The price she requires is the inherent risk of her irascible temper. She may be invoked under the sign of the archer, with the words "I am one of the ignorant, and unable to answer such an incoherent question."

The Pharisee

I never wished to love the world,
Nor yet to know the sky.
I waited when the flag unfurled,
And watched its bearer die.

I sat in silence, counting days
Like echoes in the hall.
As many did, I gave him praise
But didn't stop his fall.

He told me he could teach the art
The world was built upon.
And yet, within my secret heart,
I smiled when he was gone.

Divination
and
Prophecy

The Oracle

1: Seek out darkness and silence.

2: Journey to the Borderlands and seek out your answer as if on quest.

3: Drift on the river of sleep but keep your question in mind.

4: Hear what the voices tell you; see what you see.

"Everything that can be annihilated must be annihilated."
-William Blake

Greed

I hungered for the silver light
Of those who walk the moon.
They never showed their wings that night
Or else they came too soon.

I hungered for the sudden tears
That meant the sun was mine.
I waited for a hundred years,
But missed the proper time.

On bended knee I sought the source
Of all that moves above,
And only when I knew remorse
Decided it was love.

Divination by the Bones

When you have received a communication from Onei but are uncertain of the interpretation. Take the astragaloi in hand and roll the bones four times with offerings and incense.

When a bone lands on a convex side the answer is favorable, and when a bone lands on a concave side the answer is unfavorable. Four favorable throws tells you that your interpretation is absolutely correct, while four unfavorable throws indicates that you have misunderstood the communication. When the results are mixed, the answer is mixed in the same proportion.

The Armadel

1: prepare a chalice, a cauldron, or a pool filled with clear, cold water.

2: set up the statue of your god so that it reflects in the water, or set up a candle or other flame.

3: burn incense appropriate to the gods.

4: circumambulate the water nine times with prayer.

To the blue open heavens I pray,
And the fire at their heart I adore.
The moon, with its reflected light
Receives my love as wave-crests white
Come crashing in to shore.

To the lash of the lightning I pray,
And the gleam of the sun's bright rays.
To all the rushing rivers wide
That roar down from the mountainside,
I offer thanks and praise.

I pray to all of the distant stars
And the planets that silently roam.
I praise the earth beneath my feat
I praise the worms who will come to eat
When I at last go home.

5: stand before the water and make an offering to the Keeper of the Gate

Phantoms of the forest gather
In the shadows of the trees.
Hidden voices whisper, whisper.
I have come for all of these.

Praises to the guardian spirit,
Keeper of the in-between.
There are ways that I must wander,
And you know what ways I mean.

Here beneath the bone-white birches
And the blue-green spruce and pine
I have brought you bowls of chicken,
Goblets filled with rich red wine.

Spirit of the borders, hear me.
Throw the doors of twilight wide.
Tell the skulls that guard the pillars,
Grant me leave to pass inside.

6: gaze into the reflections in the water until you see the Keeper. Once the Keeper has arrived, ask him to welcome the gods to the feast.

7: once the gods have arrived, ask the Keeper to serve them a splendid banquet with every kind of food and drink.

This hungry pit shall open wide
And gorge on meat and wine.
These flames will burn as night-clouds turn
To watch this work of mine.

This shaft will gape so none escapes
Its toothless maw tonight.
While blue-white stars look down in awe
To see the flames so bright.

Oh gods of endless space and sky,
Oh gods of underneath,
Oh gods who live and gods who die
And gods who wait beneath,

Accept these morsels from my hand,
Drink deep and eat your fill.
I seek no benefits tonight
Unless you share my will.

8: while the gods are eating, ask the Keeper if any of them will answer your questions. If the answer is yes, ask the Keeper to bring the god to speak with you.

9: ask the god what you want to ask, and respectfully note the answer.

10: thank the Keeper and the gods and bid them farewell.

Priest, Sage, or Magician

If you cross the starry river
In the plains of day and night
You will find the priests who live there
And they'll feed you wrong and right.

Though the wrong is sour as poison
And the right is vile and sweet,
In the world of prayer and wisdom
There is nothing else to eat.

So you'll cross the deep blue desert
To the cliffs of saint and sage,
Where they'll fit you for a hair-shirt
And they'll hang you from a cage.

Though you pray until you're witless
You will never pierce the veil.
Once you're whittled down to shavings
They will tell you that you failed.

So your purview isn't wisdom-
There are other ways to be.
Ask the spiders in their burrows.
Ask the water in the sea.

In the ruined walls of Carthage
There's a man who sits alone.
He can tell you what your dream is
From the cracks along a bone.

In the Empty Quarter, keening,
There's a woman, old and blind,
And her milky eyes are staring
Through Saharas of the mind.

They will show you how to do things-
How to rule the wind and storm.
And you'll find yourself a stranger
In the place where you were born.

A Journey to Onei (7)

I was driven to shore by mighty storms, by funnels of raging water, by walls of wind. I fled them thoughtlessly, so overcome by wordless fear that I could not even remember what I once had read about the storms of Onei. It had been many years since I had opened the Book of Onei in any case, though it rode with me in my bag as I sailed. Now I lay on the shore, clutching the book to my chest like an infant. The Ship of Stars had been smashed to pieces, though that was a fact of little consequence.

I could remember who I was, but only when I made an effort to think about it. I had followed the light, searching the waters of the First Darkness, yet I could never catch up with it. When the storms came in at me, leaving me no hope of escape from the waters, I drove in panic toward a lighthouse. Or what I had imagined to be a lighthouse. Now the Ship was in splinters, and I was all alone on an empty shore.

The light had vanished, but I heard the waves and I heard a whispering. I knew I must have arrived somewhere, but I did not know where. I knew only that there were voices nearby, and that where there were voices there must be life.

I got to my feet, clutching the Book of Onei. My limbs were sore, but I was able to make them move with effort. I climbed the ridge, pulling myself up by branches when I had to. At the top of the first rise I found the pilgrims—a procession of perhaps two dozen, whispering. They seemed to have waited there for me specifically, so I nodded acknowledgment and joined their ranks. We set off, marching stoically toward some spot in the mountains.

I felt no need to join in their whispered speech. I merely walked, keeping my head down like a prayerful penitent. I glanced upward when I glimpsed a light, flickering orange and black against the outline of a temple. I saw a pile of skulls, stacked up in pyramid shape. They spoke prophesies that contradicted each other, and each was equally convincing.

We walked for hours, deeper and deeper into the wooded mountains. As time dripped by, the trees became fewer and their branches more stunted – like twisted and knotted limbs, like grasping hands. At last they stopped, and we walked on together through a treeless moonscape.

I had scarcely been conscious of the whispers around me, but I noticed them now as we climbed the ridge. My companions were not talking to each other, as I had first believed. Instead, they were talking to themselves. Each one was different, and yet all were the same in the end. All were equally alone.

I never told her. I never told her.

He won't be able to make it without me.

I'll never see them again. My little ones!

The voices chilled me, but less than the sight at the end of the path. A man was there, and I realized now that he had led the procession. He had no face, or his face was obscured by the depth of shadows. He wore a top hat and held a cane, and he gestured grandly for us to look to our right.

The gasp of fear was like a wave, spreading from the front to the back of the procession. I turned and saw, and the fear in my voice was as desperate as any. Our guide was leading us into an empty valley, so vast and dark and deep that it disappeared into utter blackness after only a few steps. He bowed grandly and pointed down, telling us without words that this Abyss was our destination.

He gestured again, but the enthusiasm he mimed seemed almost ironic. Go on! He seemed to say. Step on down into the dark! What is there for you up here? For any of you?

A second wave of sound swept through us. Some moaned in terror, others protested with feeble words.

I won't go! I will not go!

He turned to me, and I felt that he saw me although he had no eyes that I could see. I glanced down into the Pit, and then back to him. He cocked his head as if to ask a question. I nodded silently, and he nodded back as if with respect.

And then I walked down into the darkness.

Christopher Scott Thompson

is an anarchist, martial arts instructor, and devotee of Brighid and Macha. He is also the author of *Pagan Anarchism* and *If In Ruins We Must Live*

Ritona

Ritona is an imprint of Ritona a.s.b.l.// Gods&Radicals Press. Named for the Treverii goddess of river crossings, we are a non-profit publishing organisation advocating for plurality, tolerance, and respect for Pagan, Indigenous, and non-industrial ways of being in the world.

Find our online journal and book catalog at

ABEAUTIFULRESISTANCE.ORG